CA

M000014593

by

PROSPER MÉRIMÉE

COMPASS CIRCLE

Carmen.
Written by Prosper Mérimée.
Translated by Lady Mary Lloyd.
Current edition published by Compass Circle in 2019.

Published by Compass Circle
A Division of Garcia & Kitzinger Pty Ltd
Cover copyright ©2019 by Compass Circle.

Note:
All efforts have been made to preserve original spellings and punctuation of the original edition which may include old-fashioned English spellings of words and archaic variants.

This book is a product of its time and does not reflect the same views on race, gender, sexuality, ethnicity, and interpersonal relations as it would if it were written today.

For information contact :
information@compass-circle.com

I'll follow you, even to death—but I won't live with you any more.

PROSPER MÉRIMÉE

SECRET WISDOM OF THE AGES SERIES

Life presents itself, it advances in a fast way. Life indeed never stops. It never stops until the end. The most diverse questions peek and fade in our minds. Sometimes we seek for answers. Sometimes we just let time go by.

The book you have now in your hands has been waiting to be discovered by you. This book may reveal the answers to some of your questions.

Books are friends. Friends who are always by your side and who can give you great ideas, advice or just comfort your soul.

A great book can make you see things in your soul that you have not yet discovered, make you see things in your soul that you were not aware of.

Great books can change your life for the better. They can make you understand fascinating theories, give you new ideas, inspire you to undertake new challenges or to walk along new paths.

Literature Classics like the one of *Carmen* are indeed a secret to many, but for those of us lucky enough to have discovered them, by one way or another, these books can enlighten us. They can open a wide range of possibilities to us. Because achieving greatness requires knowledge.

The series SECRET WISDOM OF THE AGES presented by Compass Circle try to bring you the great timeless masterpieces of literature, autobiographies and personal development,.

We welcome you to discover with us fascinating works by Nathaniel Hawthorne, Sir Arthur Conan Doyle, Edith Wharton, among others.

CHAPTER I

I had always suspected the geographical authorities did not know what they were talking about when they located the battlefield of Munda in the county of the Bastuli-Poeni, close to the modern Monda, some two leagues north of Marbella.

According to my own surmise, founded on the text of the anonymous author of the *Bellum Hispaniense*, and on certain information culled from the excellent library owned by the Duke of Ossuna, I believed the site of the memorable struggle in which Caesar played double or quits, once and for all, with the champions of the Republic, should be sought in the neighbourhood of Montilla.

Happening to be in Andalusia during the autumn of 1830, I made a somewhat lengthy excursion, with the object of clearing up certain doubts which still oppressed me. A paper which I shall shortly publish will, I trust, remove any hesitation that may still exist in the minds of all honest archaeologists. But before that dissertation of mine finally settles the geographical problem on the solution of which the whole of learned Europe hangs, I desire to relate a little tale. It will do no prejudice to the interesting question of the correct locality of Monda.

I had hired a guide and a couple of horses at Cordova, and had started on my way with no luggage save a few shirts, and Caesar's *Commentaries*. As I wandered, one day, across the higher lands of the Cachena plain, worn with fatigue, parched with thirst, scorched by a burning sun, cursing Caesar and Pompey's sons alike, most heartily, my eye lighted, at some distance from the path I was following, on a little stretch of green sward dotted with reeds and rushes. That betokened the neighbourhood of some spring, and, indeed, as I drew nearer I perceived that what had looked like sward was a marsh, into which a stream, which seemed to issue from a narrow gorge between two high spurs of the Sierra di Cabra, ran and disappeared.

If I rode up that stream, I argued, I was likely to find cooler water, fewer leeches and frogs, and mayhap a little shade among the rocks.

At the mouth of the gorge, my horse neighed, and another horse, invisible to me, neighed back. Before I had advanced a hundred paces, the gorge suddenly widened, and I beheld a sort of natural amphitheatre, thoroughly shaded by the steep cliffs that lay all around it. It was impossible to imagine any more delightful halting place for a traveller. At the foot of the precipitous rocks, the stream bubbled upward and fell into a little basin, lined with sand that was as white as snow. Five or six splendid evergreen oaks, sheltered from the wind, and cooled by the spring, grew beside the pool, and shaded it with their thick foliage. And round about it a close and glossy turf offered the wanderer a better bed than he could have found in any hostelry for ten leagues round.

The honour of discovering this fair spot did not belong to me. A man was resting there already—sleeping, no doubt—before I reached it. Roused by the neighing of the horses, he had risen to his feet and had moved over to his mount, which had been taking advantage of its master's slumbers to make a hearty feed on the grass that grew around. He was an active young fellow, of middle height, but powerful in build, and proud and sullen-looking in expression. His complexion, which may once have been fine, had been tanned by the sun till it was darker than his hair. One of his hands grasped his horse's halter. In the other he held a brass blunderbuss.

At the first blush, I confess, the blunderbuss, and the savage looks of the man who bore it, somewhat took me aback. But I had heard so much about robbers, that, never seeing any, I had ceased to believe in their existence. And further, I had seen so many honest farmers arm themselves to the teeth before they went out to market, that the sight of firearms gave me no warrant for doubting the character of any stranger. "And then," quoth I to myself, "what could he do with my shirts and my Elzevir edition of Caesar's *Commentaries?*" So I bestowed a friendly nod on the man with the blunderbuss, and inquired, with a smile, whether I had disturbed his nap. Without any answer, he looked me over from head to foot. Then, as if the scrutiny had satisfied him, he looked as closely at my guide, who was just coming up. I saw the guide turn pale, and pull up with an air of evident alarm. "An unlucky meeting!" thought I to myself. But prudence instantly counselled me not to let any symptom of anxiety escape me. So I dismounted. I told the guide to take off the horses' bridles, and kneeling down beside the spring, I laved my head and hands and then drank a long draught, lying flat on my belly, like Gideon's soldiers.

Meanwhile, I watched the stranger, and my own guide. This last seemed to come forward unwillingly. But the other did not appear to have any evil designs upon us. For he had turned his horse loose, and the blunderbuss, which he had been holding horizontally, was now dropped earthward.

Not thinking it necessary to take offence at the scant attention paid me, I stretched myself full length upon the grass, and calmly asked the owner of the blunderbuss whether he had a light about him. At the same time I pulled out my cigar-case. The stranger, still without opening his lips, took out his flint, and lost no time in getting me a light. He was evidently growing tamer, for he sat down opposite to me, though he still grasped his weapon. When I had lighted my cigar, I chose out the best I had left, and asked him whether he smoked.

"Yes, señor," he replied. These were the first words I had heard him speak, and I noticed that he did not pronounce the letter s[1] in the Andalusian fashion, whence I concluded he was a traveller, like myself, though, maybe, somewhat less of an archaeologist.

"You'll find this a fairly good one," said I, holding out a real Havana regalia.

He bowed his head slightly, lighted his cigar at mine, thanked me with another nod, and began to smoke with a most lively appearance of enjoyment.

"Ah!" he exclaimed, as he blew his first puff of smoke slowly out of his ears and nostrils. "What a time it is since I've had a smoke!"

In Spain the giving and accepting of a cigar establishes bonds of hospitality similar to those founded in Eastern countries on the partaking of bread and salt. My friend turned out more talkative than I had hoped. However, though he claimed to belong to the *partido* of Montilla, he seemed very ill-informed about the country. He did not know the name of the delightful valley in which we were sitting, he could not tell me the names of any of the neighbouring

---

[1] The Andalusians aspirate the s, and pronounce it like the soft c and the z, which Spaniards pronounce like the English th. An Andalusian may always be recognised by the way in which he says señor.

villages, and when I inquired whether he had not noticed any broken-down walls, broad-rimmed tiles, or carved stones in the vicinity, he confessed he had never paid any heed to such matters. On the other hand, he showed himself an expert in horseflesh, found fault with my mount—not a difficult affair—and gave me a pedigree of his own, which had come from the famous stud at Cordova. It was a splendid creature, indeed, so tough, according to its owner's claim, that it had once covered thirty leagues in one day, either at the gallop or at full trot the whole time. In the midst of his story the stranger pulled up short, as if startled and sorry he had said so much. "The fact is I was in a great hurry to get to Cordova," he went on, somewhat embarrassed. "I had to petition the judges about a lawsuit." As he spoke, he looked at my guide Antonio, who had dropped his eyes.

The spring and the cool shade were so delightful that I bethought me of certain slices of an excellent ham, which my friends at Montilla had packed into my guide's wallet. I bade him produce them, and invited the stranger to share our impromptu lunch. If he had not smoked for a long time, he certainly struck me as having fasted for eight-and-forty hours at the very least. He ate like a starving wolf, and I thought to myself that my appearance must really have been quite providential for the poor fellow. Meanwhile my guide ate but little, drank still less, and spoke never a word, although in the earlier part of our journey he had proved himself a most unrivalled chatterer. He seemed ill at ease in the presence of our guest, and a sort of mutual distrust, the cause of which I could not exactly fathom, seemed to be between them.

The last crumbs of bread and scraps of ham had disappeared. We had each smoked our second cigar; I told the guide to bridle the horses, and was just about to take leave of my new friend, when he inquired where I was going to spend the night.

Before I had time to notice a sign my guide was making to me I had replied that I was going to the Venta del Cuervo.

"That's a bad lodging for a gentleman like you, sir! I'm bound there myself, and if you'll allow me to ride with you, we'll go together."

"With pleasure!" I replied, mounting my horse. The guide, who was holding my stirrup, looked at me meaningly again. I answered by shrugging my shoulders, as though to assure him I was perfectly easy in my mind, and we started on our way.

Antonio's mysterious signals, his evident anxiety, a few words dropped by the stranger, above all, his ride of thirty leagues, and the far from plausible explanation he had given us of it, had already enabled me to form an opinion as to the identity of my fellow-traveller. I had no doubt at all I was in the company of a smuggler, and possibly of a brigand. What cared I? I knew enough of the Spanish character to be very certain I had nothing to fear from a man who had eaten and smoked with me. His very presence would protect me in case of any undesirable meeting. And besides, I was very glad to know what a brigand was really like. One doesn't come across such gentry every day. And there is a certain charm about finding one's self in close proximity to a dangerous being, especially when one feels the being in question to be gentle and tame.

I was hoping the stranger might gradually fall into a confidential mood, and in spite of my guide's winks, I turned the conversation to the subject of highwaymen. I need scarcely say that I spoke of them with great respect. At that time there was a famous brigand in Andalusia, of the name of Jose-Maria, whose exploits were on every lip. "Supposing I should be riding along with Jose-Maria!" said I to myself. I told all the stories I knew about the hero—they were all to his credit, indeed, and loudly expressed my admiration of his generosity and his valour.

"Jose-Maria is nothing but a blackguard," said the stranger gravely.

"Is he just to himself, or is this an excess of modesty?" I queried, mentally, for by dint of scrutinizing my companion, I had ended by reconciling his appearance with the description of Jose-Maria which

I read posted up on the gates of various Andalusian towns. "Yes, this must be he—fair hair, blue eyes, large mouth, good teeth, small hands, fine shirt, a velvet jacket with silver buttons on it, white leather gaiters, and a bay horse. Not a doubt about it. But his *incognito* shall be respected!" We reached the *venta*. It was just what he had described to me. In other words, the most wretched hole of its kind I had as yet beheld. One large apartment served as kitchen, dining-room, and sleeping chamber. A fire was burning on a flat stone in the middle of the room, and the smoke escaped through a hole in the roof, or rather hung in a cloud some feet above the soil. Along the walls five or six mule rugs were spread on the floor. These were the travellers' beds. Twenty paces from the house, or rather from the solitary apartment which I have just described, stood a sort of shed, that served for a stable.

The only inhabitants of this delightful dwelling visible at the moment, at all events, were an old woman, and a little girl of ten or twelve years old, both of them as black as soot, and dressed in loathsome rags. "Here's the sole remnant of the ancient populations of Munda Boetica," said I to myself. "O Caesar! O Sextus Pompeius, if you were to revisit this earth how astounded you would be!"

When the old woman saw my travelling companion an exclamation of surprise escaped her. "Ah!

Señor Don Jose!" she cried.

Don Jose frowned and lifted his hand with a gesture of authority that forthwith silenced the old dame.

I turned to my guide and gave him to understand, by a sign that no one else perceived, that I knew all about the man in whose company I was about to spend the night. Our supper was better than I expected. On a little table, only a foot high, we were served with an old rooster, fricasseed with rice and numerous peppers, then more peppers in oil, and finally a *gaspacho*—a sort of salad made of peppers. These three highly spiced dishes involved our frequent recourse to a goatskin filled with Montella wine, which struck us as being delicious.

After our meal was over, I caught sight of a mandolin hanging up against the wall—in Spain you see mandolins in every corner—and I asked the little girl, who had been waiting on us, if she knew how to play it.

"No," she replied. "But Don Jose does play well!"

"Do me the kindness to sing me something," I said to him, "I'm passionately fond of your national music."

"I can't refuse to do anything for such a charming gentleman, who gives me such excellent cigars," responded Don Jose gaily, and having made the child give him the mandolin, he sang to his own accompaniment. His voice, though rough, was pleasing, the air he sang was strange and sad. As to the words, I could not understand a single one of them.

"If I am not mistaken," said I, "that's not a Spanish air you have just been singing. It's like the *zorzicos* I've heard in the Provinces,[2] and the words must be in the Basque language."

"Yes," said Don Jose, with a gloomy look. He laid the mandolin down on the ground, and began staring with a peculiarly sad expression at the dying fire. His face, at once fierce and noble-looking, reminded me, as the firelight fell on it, of Milton's Satan. Like him, perchance, my comrade was musing over the home he had forfeited, the exile he had earned, by some misdeed. I tried to revive the conversation, but so absorbed was he in melancholy thought, that he gave me no answer.

The old woman had already gone to rest in a corner of the room, behind a ragged rug hung on a rope. The little girl had followed her into this retreat, sacred to the fair sex. Then my guide rose, and suggested that I should go with him to the stable. But at the word Don Jose, waking, as it were, with a start, inquired sharply whither he was going.

"To the stable," answered the guide.

"What for? The horses have been fed! You can sleep here. The señor will give you leave."

---

[2]The *privileged Provinces*, Alava, Biscay, Guipuzcoa, and a part of Navarre, which all enjoy special *fueros*. The Basque language is spoken in these countries.

"I'm afraid the señor's horse is sick. I'd like the señor to see it. Perhaps he'd know what should be done for it."

It was quite clear to me that Antonio wanted to speak to me apart.

But I did not care to rouse Don Jose's suspicions, and being as we were, I thought far the wisest course for me was to appear absolutely confident.

I therefore told Antonio that I knew nothing on earth about horses, and that I was desperately sleepy. Don Jose followed him to the stable, and soon returned alone. He told me there was nothing the matter with the horse, but that my guide considered the animal such a treasure that he was scrubbing it with his jacket to make it sweat, and expected to spend the night in that pleasing occupation. Meanwhile I had stretched myself out on the mule rugs, having carefully wrapped myself up in my own cloak, so as to avoid touching them. Don Jose, having begged me to excuse the liberty he took in placing himself so near me, lay down across the door, but not until he had primed his blunderbuss afresh and carefully laid it under the wallet, which served him as a pillow.

I had thought I was so tired that I should be able to sleep even in such a lodging. But within an hour a most unpleasant itching sensation roused me from my first nap. As soon as I realized its nature, I rose to my feet, feeling convinced I should do far better to spend the rest of the night in the open air than beneath that inhospitable roof. Walking tiptoe I reached the door, stepped over Don Jose, who was sleeping the sleep of the just, and managed so well that I got outside the building without waking him. Just beside the door there was a wide wooden bench. I lay down upon it, and settled myself, as best I could, for the remainder of the night. I was just closing my eyes for a second time when I fancied I saw the shadow of a man and then the shadow of a horse moving absolutely noiselessly, one behind the other. I sat upright, and then I thought I recognised Antonio. Surprised to see him outside the stable at such an hour, I got up and went toward him. He had seen me first, and had stopped to wait for me.

"Where is he?" Antonio inquired in a low tone.

"In the *venta*. He's asleep. The bugs don't trouble him. But what are you going to do with that horse?" I then noticed that, to stifle all noise as he moved out of the shed, Antonio had carefully muffled the horse's feet in the rags of an old blanket.

"Speak lower, for God's sake," said Antonio. "You don't know who that man is. He's Jose Navarro, the most noted bandit in Andalusia. I've been making signs to you all day long, and you wouldn't understand."

"What do I care whether he's a brigand or not," I replied. "He hasn't robbed us, and I'll wager he doesn't want to."

"That may be. But there are two hundred ducats on his head. Some lancers are stationed in a place I know, a league and a half from here, and before daybreak I'll bring a few brawny fellows back with me. I'd have taken his horse away, but the brute's so savage that nobody but Navarro can go near it."

"Devil take you!" I cried. "What harm has the poor fellow done you that you should want to inform against him? And besides, are you certain he is the brigand you take him for?"

"Perfectly certain! He came after me into the stable just now, and said, 'You seem to know me. If you tell that good gentleman who I am, I'll blow your brains out!' You stay here, sir, keep close to him. You've nothing to fear. As long as he knows you are there, he won't suspect anything."

As we talked, we had moved so far from the *venta* that the noise of the horse's hoofs could not be heard there. In a twinkling Antonio snatched off the rags he had wrapped around the creature's feet, and was just about to climb on its back. In vain did I attempt with prayers and threats to restrain him.

"I'm only a poor man, señor," quoth he, "I can't afford to lose two hundred ducats—especially when I shall earn them by ridding the country of such vermin. But mind what you're about! If Navarro wakes up, he'll snatch at his blunderbuss, and then look out for yourself! I've gone too far now to turn back. Do the best you can for yourself!"

The villain was in his saddle already, he spurred his horse smartly, and I soon lost sight of them both in the darkness.

I was very angry with my guide, and terribly alarmed as well. After a moment's reflection, I made up my mind, and went back to the *venta*. Don Jose was still sound asleep, making up, no doubt, for the fatigue and sleeplessness of several days of adventure. I had to shake him roughly before I could wake him up. Never shall I forget his fierce look, and the spring he made to get hold of his blunderbuss, which, as a precautionary measure, I had removed to some distance from his couch.

"Señor," I said, "I beg your pardon for disturbing you. But I have a silly question to ask you. Would you be glad to see half a dozen lancers walk in here?"

He bounded to his feet, and in an awful voice he demanded:

"Who told you?"

"It's little matter whence the warning comes, so long as it be good."

"Your guide has betrayed me—but he shall pay for it! Where is he?"

"I don't know. In the stable, I fancy. But somebody told me—"

"Who told you? It can't be the old hag—"

"Some one I don't know. Without more parleying, tell me, yes or no, have you any reason for not waiting till the soldiers come? If you have any, lose no time! If not, good-night to you, and forgive me for having disturbed your slumbers!"

"Ah, your guide! Your guide! I had my doubts of him at first—but—I'll settle with him! Farewell, señor. May God reward you for the service I owe you! I am not quite so wicked as you think me. Yes, I still have something in me that an honest man may pity. Farewell, señor! I have only one regret—that I can not pay my debt to you!"

"As a reward for the service I have done you, Don Jose, promise me you'll suspect nobody—nor seek for vengeance. Here are some cigars for your journey. Good luck to you." And I held out my hand to him.

He squeezed it, without a word, took up his wallet and blunderbuss, and after saying a few words to the old woman in a lingo that I could not understand, he ran out to the shed. A few minutes later, I heard him galloping out into the country.

As for me, I lay down again on my bench, but I did not go to sleep again. I queried in my own mind whether I had done right to save a robber, and possibly a murderer, from the gallows, simply and solely because I had eaten ham and rice in his company. Had I not betrayed my guide, who was supporting the cause of law and order? Had I not exposed him to a ruffian's vengeance? But then, what about the laws of hospitality?

"A mere savage prejudice," said I to myself. "I shall have to answer for all the crimes this brigand may commit in future." Yet is that instinct of the conscience which resists every argument really a prejudice? It may be I could not have escaped from the delicate position in which I found myself without remorse of some kind. I was still tossed to and fro, in the greatest uncertainty as to the morality of my behaviour, when I saw half a dozen horsemen ride up, with Antonio prudently lagging behind them. I went to meet them, and told them the brigand had fled over two hours previously. The old woman, when she was questioned by the sergeant, admitted that she knew Navarro, but said that living alone, as she did, she would never have dared to risk her life by informing against him. She added that when he came to her house, he habitually went away in the middle of the night. I, for my part, was made to ride to a place some leagues away, where I showed my passport, and signed a declaration before the *Alcalde*. This done, I was allowed to recommence my archaeological investigations. Antonio was sulky with me; suspecting it was I who had prevented his earning those two hundred ducats. Nevertheless, we parted good friends at Cordova, where I gave him as large a gratuity as the state of my finances would permit.

CHAPTER II

I spent several days at Cordova. I had been told of a
certain manuscript in the library of the Dominican
convent which was likely to furnish me with very
interesting details about the ancient Munda. The
good fathers gave me the most kindly welcome. I
spent the daylight hours within their convent, and
at night I walked about the town. At Cordova a great
many idlers collect, toward sunset, in the quay that
runs along the right bank of the Guadalquivir. Prom-
enaders on the spot have to breathe the odour of
a tan yard which still keeps up the ancient fame of
the country in connection with the curing of leather.
But to atone for this, they enjoy a sight which has a
charm of its own. A few minutes before the Angelus
bell rings, a great company of women gathers beside
the river, just below the quay, which is rather a high
one. Not a man would dare to join its ranks. The
moment the Angelus rings, darkness is supposed to
have fallen. As the last stroke sounds, all the women
disrobe and step into the water. Then there is laughing and screaming and a wonderful clatter. The men
on the upper quay watch the bathers, straining their
eyes, and seeing very little. Yet the white uncertain

18

outlines perceptible against the dark-blue waters of the stream stir the poetic mind, and the possessor of a little fancy finds it not difficult to imagine that Diana and her nymphs are bathing below, while he himself runs no risk of ending like Acteon.

I have been told that one day a party of good-for-nothing fellows banded themselves together, and bribed the bell-ringer at the cathedral to ring the Angelus some twenty minutes before the proper hour. Though it was still broad daylight, the nymphs of the Guadalquivir never hesitated, and putting far more trust in the Angelus bell than in the sun, they proceeded to their bathing toilette—always of the simplest—with an easy conscience. I was not present on that occasion. In my day, the bell-ringer was incorruptible, the twilight was very dim, and nobody but a cat could have distinguished the difference between the oldest orange woman, and the prettiest shop-girl, in Cordova.

One evening, after it had grown quite dusk, I was leaning over the parapet of the quay, smoking, when a woman came up the steps leading from the river, and sat down near me. In her hair she wore a great bunch of jasmine—a flower which, at night, exhales a most intoxicating perfume. She was dressed simply, almost poorly, in black, as most work-girls are dressed in the evening. Women of the richer class only wear black in the daytime, at night they dress *a la francesa*. When she drew near me, the woman let the mantilla which had covered her head drop on her shoulders, and "by the dim light falling from the stars" I perceived her to be young, short in stature, well-proportioned, and with very large eyes. I threw my cigar away at once. She appreciated this mark of courtesy, essentially French, and hastened to inform me that she was very fond of the smell of tobacco, and that she even smoked herself, when she could get very mild *papelitos*. I fortunately happened to have some such in my case, and at once offered them to her. She condescended to take one, and lighted it at a burning string which a child brought us, receiving a copper for its pains. We mingled our smoke, and talked so long, the fair lady and I, that we ended by being almost alone on the quay. I thought I might venture, without impropriety, to suggest our going to eat an ice at the *neveria*.[1] After a moment of modest demur, she agreed. But before finally accepting, she desired to know what o'clock it was. I struck my repeater, and this seemed to astound her greatly.

"What clever inventions you foreigners do have! What country do you belong to, sir? You're an Englishman, no doubt!"[2]

"I'm a Frenchman, and your devoted servant. And

---

[1] A café to which a depot of ice, or rather of snow, is attached. There is hardly a village in Spain without its neveria.

[2] Every traveller in Spain who does not carry about samples of calicoes and silks is taken for an Englishman (inglesito). It is the same thing in the East.

you, señora, or señorita, you probably belong to Cordova?"

"No."

"At all events, you are an Andalusian? Your soft way of speaking makes me think so."

"If you notice people's accent so closely, you must be able to guess what I am."

"I think you are from the country of Jesus, two paces out of Paradise."

I had learned the metaphor, which stands for Andalusia, from my friend Francisco Sevilla, a well-known *picador*.

"Pshaw! The people here say there is no place in Paradise for us!"

"Then perhaps you are of Moorish blood—or——" I stopped, not venturing to add "a Jewess."

"Oh come! You must see I'm a gipsy! Wouldn't you like me to tell you *la baji*?[3] Did you never hear tell of Carmencita? That's who I am!"

I was such a miscreant in those days—now fifteen years ago—that the close proximity of a sorceress did not make me recoil in horror. "So be it!" I thought. "Last week I ate my supper with a highway robber. To-day I'll go and eat ices with a servant of the devil. A traveller should see everything." I had yet another motive for prosecuting her acquaintance. When I left college—I acknowledge it with shame—I had wasted

---

[3] Your fortune.

21

a certain amount of time in studying occult science, and had even attempted, more than once, to exorcise the powers of darkness. Though I had been cured, long since, of my passion for such investigations, I still felt a certain attraction and curiosity with regard to all superstitions, and I was delighted to have this opportunity of discovering how far the magic art had developed among the gipsies.

Talking as we went, we had reached the *neveria*, and seated ourselves at a little table, lighted by a taper protected by a glass globe. I then had time to take a leisurely view of my *gitana*, while several worthy individuals, who were eating their ices, stared open-mouthed at beholding me in such gay company.

I very much doubt whether Señorita Carmen was a pure-blooded gipsy. At all events, she was infinitely prettier than any other woman of her race I have ever seen. For a women to be beautiful, they say in Spain, she must fulfil thirty *ifs*, or, if it please you better, you must be able to define her appearance by ten adjectives, applicable to three portions of her person.

For instance, three things about her must be black, her eyes, her eyelashes, and her eyebrows. Three must be dainty, her fingers, her lips, her hair, and so forth. For the rest of this inventory, see Brantome. My gipsy girl could lay no claim to so many perfections. Her skin, though perfectly smooth, was almost of a copper hue. Her eyes were set obliquely in her head, but they were magnificent and large. Her lips, a little full, but beautifully shaped, revealed a set of teeth as white as newly skinned almonds. Her hair—a trifle coarse, perhaps—was black, with blue lights on it like a raven's wing, long and glossy. Not to weary my readers with too prolix a description, I will merely add, that to every blemish she united some advantage, which was perhaps all the more evident by contrast. There was something strange and wild about her beauty. Her face astonished you, at first sight, but nobody could forget it. Her eyes, especially, had an expression of mingled sensuality and fierceness which I had never seen in any other human glance. "Gipsy's eye, wolf's eye!" is a Spanish saying which denotes close observation. If my readers have no time to go to the "Jardin des Plantes" to study the wolf's expression, they will do well to watch the ordinary cat when it is lying in wait for a sparrow.

It will be understood that I should have looked ridiculous if I had proposed to have my fortune told in a *café*. I therefore begged the pretty witch's leave to go home with her. She made no difficulties about consenting, but she wanted to know what o'clock it was again, and requested me to make my repeater strike once more.

"Is it really gold?" she said, gazing at it with rapt

attention.

When we started off again, it was quite dark. Most of the shops were shut, and the streets were almost empty. We crossed the bridge over the Guadalquivir, and at the far end of the suburb we stopped in front of a house of anything but palatial appearance. The door was opened by a child, to whom the gipsy spoke a few words in a language unknown to me, which I afterward understood to be *Romany*, or *chipe calli*— the gipsy idiom. The child instantly disappeared, leaving us in sole possession of a tolerably spacious room, furnished with a small table, two stools, and a chest. I must not forget to mention a jar of water, a pile of oranges, and a bunch of onions.

As soon as we were left alone, the gipsy produced, out of her chest, a pack of cards, bearing signs of constant usage, a magnet, a dried chameleon, and a few other indispensable adjuncts of her art. Then she bade me cross my left hand with a silver coin, and the magic ceremonies duly began. It is unnecessary to chronicle her predictions, and as for the style of her performance, it proved her to be no mean sorceress.

Unluckily we were soon disturbed. The door was suddenly burst open, and a man, shrouded to the eyes in a brown cloak, entered the room, apostrophizing the gipsy in anything but gentle terms. What he said I could not catch, but the tone of his voice revealed the fact that he was in a very evil temper.

The gipsy betrayed neither surprise nor anger at his advent, but she ran to meet him, and with a most striking volubility, she poured out several sentences in the mysterious language she had already used in my presence. The word *payllo*, frequently reiterated, was the only one I understood. I knew that the gipsies use it to describe all men not of their own race. Concluding myself to be the subject of this discourse, I was prepared for a somewhat delicate explanation. I had already laid my hand on the leg of one of the stools, and was studying within myself to discover the exact moment at which I had better throw it at his head, when, roughly pushing the gipsy to one side, the man advanced toward me. Then with a step backward he cried:

"What, sir! Is it you?"

I looked at him in my turn and recognised my friend Don Jose. At that moment I did feel rather sorry I had saved him from the gallows.

"What, is it you, my good fellow?" I exclaimed, with as easy a smile as I could muster. "You have interrupted this young lady just when she was foretelling me most interesting things!"

"The same as ever. There shall be an end to it!" he hissed between his teeth, with a savage glance at her.

Meanwhile the *gitana* was still talking to him in her own tongue. She became more and more excited. Her eyes grew fierce and bloodshot, her features contracted, she stamped her foot. She seemed to me to be earnestly pressing him to do something he was unwilling to do. What this was I fancied I understood only too well, by the fashion in which she kept drawing her little hand backward and forward under her chin. I was inclined to think she wanted to have somebody's throat cut, and I had a fair suspicion the throat in question was my own. To all her torrent of eloquence Don Jose's only reply was two or three shortly spoken words. At this the gipsy cast a glance of the most utter scorn at him, then, seating herself Turkish-fashion in a corner of the room, she picked out an orange, tore off the skin, and began to eat it.

Don Jose took hold of my arm, opened the door, and led me into the street. We walked some two hundred paces in the deepest silence. Then he stretched out his hand.

"Go straight on," he said, "and you'll come to the bridge."

That instant he turned his back on me and departed at a great pace. I took my way back to my inn, rather crestfallen, and considerably out of temper. The worst of all was that, when I undressed, I discovered my watch was missing.

Various considerations prevented me from going to claim it next day, or requesting the *Corregidor* to be good enough to have a search made for it. I finished my work on the Dominican manuscript, and went on to Seville. After several months spent wandering hither and thither in Andalusia, I wanted to get back to Madrid, and with that object I had to pass through Cordova. I had no intention of making any stay there, for I had taken a dislike to that fair city, and to the ladies who bathed in the Guadalquivir. Nevertheless, I had some visits to pay, and certain errands to do, which must detain me several days in the old capital of the Mussulman princes.

The moment I made my appearance in the Dominican convent, one of the monks, who had always shown the most lively interest in my inquiries as to the site of the battlefield of Munda, welcomed me with open arms, exclaiming:

"Praised be God! You are welcome! My dear friend. We all thought you were dead, and I myself have said many a *pater* and *ave* (not that I regret them!) for your soul. Then you weren't murdered, after all? That you were robbed, we know!"

"What do you mean?" I asked, rather astonished.

"Oh, you know! That splendid repeater you used to strike in the library whenever we said it was time for us to go into church. Well, it has been found, and you'll get it back."

"Why," I broke in, rather put out of countenance, "I lost it—"

"The rascal's under lock and key, and as he was known to be a man who would shoot any Christian for the sake of a *peseta*, we were most dreadfully afraid he had killed you. I'll go with you to the *Corregidor*, and he'll give you back your fine watch. And after that, you won't dare to say the law doesn't do its work properly in Spain."

"I assure you," said I, "I'd far rather lose my watch than have to give evidence in court to hang a poor unlucky devil, and especially because—because——"

"Oh, you needn't be alarmed! He's thoroughly done for; they might hang him twice over. But when I say hang, I say wrong. Your thief is an *Hidalgo*. So he's to be garrotted the day after to-morrow, without fail.[4] So you see one theft more or less won't affect his position. Would to God he had done nothing but steal! But he has committed several murders, one more hideous than the other."

"What's his name?"

"In this country he is only known as Jose Navarro, but he has another Basque name, which neither your nor I will ever be able to pronounce. By the way, the man is worth seeing, and you, who like to study the peculiar features of each country, shouldn't lose this chance of noting how a rascal bids farewell to this world in Spain. He is in jail, and Father Martinez will take you to him."

So bent was my Dominican friend on my seeing

---

[4]In 1830, the noble class still enjoyed this privilege. Nowadays, under the constitutional regime, commoners have attained the same dignity.

the preparations for this "neat little hanging job" that I was fain to agree. I went to see the prisoner, having provided myself with a bundle of cigars, which I hoped might induce him to forgive my intrusion.

I was ushered into Don Jose's presence just as he was sitting at table. He greeted me with a rather distant nod, and thanked me civilly for the present I had brought him. Having counted the cigars in the bundle I had placed in his hand, he took out a certain number and returned me the rest, remarking that he would not need any more of them.

I inquired whether by laying out a little money, or by applying to my friends, I might not be able to do something to soften his lot. He shrugged his shoulders, to begin with, smiling sadly. Soon, as by an after-thought, he asked me to have a mass said for the repose of his soul.

Then he added nervously: "Would you—would you have another said for a person who did you a wrong?"

"Assuredly I will, my dear fellow," I answered. "But no one in this country has wronged me so far as I know."

He took my hand and squeezed it, looking very grave. After a moment's silence, he spoke again.

"Might I dare to ask another service of you? When you go back to your own country perhaps you will pass through Navarre. At all events you'll go by Vittoria, which isn't very far off."

"Yes," said I, "I shall certainly pass through Vittoria. But I may very possibly go round by Pampeluna, and for your sake, I believe I should be very glad to do it."

"Well, if you do go to Pampeluna, you'll see more than one thing that will interest you. It's a fine town. I'll give you this medal," he showed me a little silver medal that he wore hung around his neck. "You'll wrap it up in paper"—he paused a moment to master his emotion—"and you'll take it, or send it, to an old lady whose address I'll give you. Tell her I am dead—but don't tell her how I died."

I promised to perform his commission. I saw him the next day, and spent part of it in his company. From his lips I learned the sad incidents that follow.

CHAPTER III

"I was born," he said, "at Elizondo, in the valley of Baztan. My name is Don Jose Lizzarrabengoa, and you know enough of Spain, sir, to know at once, by my name, that I come of an old Christian and Basque stock. I call myself Don, because I have a right to it, and if I were at Elizondo I could show you my parchment genealogy. My family wanted me to go into the church, and made me study for it, but I did not like work. I was too fond of playing tennis, and that was my ruin. When we Navarrese begin to play tennis, we forget everything else. One day, when I had won the game, a young fellow from Alava picked a quarrel with me. We took to our *maquilas*,[1] and I won again. But I had to leave the neighbourhood. I fell in with some dragoons, and enlisted in the Almanza Cavalry Regiment. Mountain folks like us soon learn to be soldiers. Before long I was a corporal, and I had been told I should soon be made a sergeant, when, to my misfortune, I was put on guard at the Seville Tobacco Factory. If you have been to Seville you have seen the great building, just outside the ramparts, close to the Guadalquivir; I

[1] Iron-shod sticks used by the Basques.

31

can fancy I see the entrance, and the guard room just beside it, even now. When Spanish soldiers are on duty, they either play cards or go to sleep. I, like an honest Navarrese, always tried to keep myself busy. I was making a chain to hold my priming-pin, out of a bit of wire: all at once, my comrades said, 'there's the bell ringing, the girls are coming back to work.' You must know, sir, that there are quite four or five hundred women employed in the factory. They roll the cigars in a great room into which no man can go without a permit from the *Veintiquatro*,[2] because when the weather is hot they make themselves at home, especially the young ones. When the work-girls come back after their dinner, numbers of young men go down to see them pass by, and talk all sorts of nonsense to them. Very few of those young ladies will refuse a silk mantilla, and men who care for that sort of sport have nothing to do but bend down and pick their fish up. While the others watched the girls go by, I stayed on my bench near the door. I was a young fellow then—my heart was still in my own country, and I didn't believe in any pretty girls who hadn't blue skirts and long plaits of hair falling on their shoulders.[3] And besides, I was rather afraid of the Andalusian women. I had not got used to their ways yet; they were always jeering one—never spoke

---

[2]Magistrate in charge of the municipal police arrangements, and local government regulations.

[3]The costume usually worn by peasant women in Navarre and the Basque Provinces.

a single word of sense. So I was sitting with my nose down upon my chain, when I heard some bystanders say, 'Here comes the *gitanella*!' Then I lifted up my eyes, and I saw her! It was that very Carmen you know, and in whose rooms I met you a few months ago.

"She was wearing a very short skirt, below which her white silk stockings—with more than one hole in them—and her dainty red morocco shoes, fastened with flame-coloured ribbons, were clearly seen. She had thrown her mantilla back, to show her shoulders, and a great bunch of acacia that was thrust into her chemise. She had another acacia blossom in the corner of her mouth, and she walked along, swaying her hips, like a filly from the Cordova stud farm. In my country anybody who had seen a woman dressed in that fashion would have crossed himself. At Seville every man paid her some bold compliment on her appearance. She had an answer for each and all, with her hand on her hip, as bold as the thorough gipsy she was. At first I didn't like her looks, and I fell to my work again. But she, like all women and cats, who won't come if you call them, and do come if you don't call them, stopped short in front of me, and spoke to me.

"'*Compadre*,' said she, in the Andalusian fashion, 'won't you give me your chain for the keys of my strong box?'

"'It's for my priming-pin,' said I.

"'Your priming-pin!' she cried, with a laugh. 'Oho! I suppose the gentleman makes lace, as he wants pins!'

"Everybody began to laugh, and I felt myself getting red in the face, and couldn't hit on anything in answer.

"'Come, my love!' she began again, 'make me seven ells of lace for my mantilla, my pet pin-maker!'

"And taking the acacia blossom out of her mouth she flipped it at me with her thumb so that it hit me just between the eyes. I tell you, sir, I felt as if a bullet had struck me. I didn't know which way to look. I sat stock-still, like a wooden board. When she had gone into the factory, I saw the acacia blossom, which had fallen on the ground between my feet. I don't know what made me do it, but I picked it up, unseen by any of my comrades, and put it carefully inside my jacket. That was my first folly.

"Two or three hours later I was still thinking about her, when a panting, terrified-looking porter rushed into the guard-room. He told us a woman had been stabbed in the great cigar-room, and that the guard must be sent in at once. The sergeant told me to take two men, and go and see to it. I took my two men and went upstairs. Imagine, sir, that when I got into the room, I found, to begin with, some three hundred women, stripped to their shifts, or very near it, all of them screaming and yelling and gesticulating, and making such a row that you couldn't have heard God's own thunder. On one side of the room one of the women was lying on the broad of her back, streaming with blood, with an X newly cut on her face by two strokes of a knife. Opposite the wounded woman, whom the best-natured of the band were attending, I saw Carmen, held by five or six of her comrades. The wounded woman was crying out, 'A confessor, a confessor! I'm killed!' Carmen said nothing at all. She clinched her teeth and rolled her eyes like a chameleon. 'What's this?' I asked. I had hard work to find out what had happened, for all the work-girls talked at once. It appeared that the injured girl had boasted she had money enough in her pocket to buy a donkey at the Triana Market. 'Why,' said Carmen, who had a tongue of her own, 'can't you do with a broom?' Stung by this taunt, it may be because she felt herself rather unsound in that particular, the other girl replied that she knew nothing about brooms, seeing she had not the honour of being either a gipsy or one of the devil's godchildren, but that the Señorita Carmen would shortly make acquaintance with her donkey, when the *Corregidor* took her out riding with two lackeys behind her to keep the flies off. 'Well,' retorted Carmen, 'I'll make troughs for the flies to drink out of on your cheeks, and I'll

paint a draught-board on them!'[4] And thereupon,
slap, bank! She began making St. Andrew's crosses
on the girl's face with a knife she had been using for
cutting off the ends of the cigars.

"The case was quite clear. I took hold of Carmen's
arm. 'Sister mine,' I said civilly, 'you must come with
me.' She shot a glance of recognition at me, but she
said, with a resigned look: 'Let's be off. Where is my
mantilla?' She put it over her head so that only one
of her great eyes was to be seen, and followed my
two men, as quiet as a lamb. When we got to the
guardroom the sergeant said it was a serious job, and
he must send her to prison. I was told off again to
take her there. I put her between two dragoons, as
a corporal does on such occasions. We started off
for the town. The gipsy had begun by holding her
tongue. But when we got to the *Calle de la Serpiente*—
you know it, and that it earns its name by its many
windings—she began by dropping her mantilla on
to her shoulders, so as to show me her coaxing little
face, and turning round to me as well as she could,
she said:

"'*Oficial mio*, where are you taking me to?'

"'To prison, my poor child,' I replied, as gently as
I could, just as any kind-hearted soldier is bound to
speak to a prisoner, and especially to a woman.

[4]Pintar un javeque, "paint a xebec," a particular type of ship.
Most Spanish vessels of this description have a checkered red and
white stripe painted around them.

"'Alack! What will become of me! Señor Oficial, have pity on me! You are so young, so good-looking.' Then, in a lower tone, she said, 'Let me get away, and I'll give you a bit of the *bar lachi*, that will make every woman fall in love with you!'

"The *bar lachi*, sir, is the loadstone, with which the gipsies declare one who knows how to use it can cast any number of spells. If you can make a woman drink a little scrap of it, powdered, in a glass of white wine, she'll never be able to resist you. I answered, as gravely as I could:

"'We are not here to talk nonsense. You'll have to go to prison. Those are my orders, and there's no help for it!'

"We men from the Basque country have an accent which all Spaniards easily recognise; on the other hand, not one of them can ever learn to say *Bai, jaona*![5]

"So Carmen easily guessed I was from the Provinces. You know, sir, that the gipsies, who belong to no particular country, and are always moving about, speak every language, and most of them are quite at home in Portugal, in France, in our Provinces, in Catalonia, or anywhere else. They can even make themselves understood by Moors and English people. Carmen knew Basque tolerably well.

"'*Laguna ene bihotsarena*, comrade of my heart,'

[5]Yes, sir.

said she suddenly. 'Do you belong to our country?'

"Our language is so beautiful, sir, that when we hear it in a foreign country it makes us quiver. I wish," added the bandit in a lower tone, "I could have a confessor from my own country."

After a silence, he began again.

"'I belong to Elizondo,' I answered in Basque, very much affected by the sound of my own language.

"'I come from Etchalar,' said she (that's a district about four hours' journey from my home). 'I was carried off to Seville by the gipsies. I was working in the factory to earn enough money to take me back to Navarre, to my poor old mother, who has no support in the world but me, besides her little *barratcea*[6] with twenty cider-apple trees in it. Ah! if I were only back in my own country, looking up at the white mountains! I have been insulted here, because I don't belong to this land of rogues and sellers of rotten oranges; and those hussies are all banded together against me, because I told them that not all their Seville *jacques*,[7] and all their knives, would frighten an honest lad from our country, with his blue cap and his *maquila*! Good comrade, won't you do anything to help your own countrywoman?'

"She was lying then, sir, as she has always lied. I don't know that that girl ever spoke a word of truth in her life, but when she did speak, I believed her—I

[6] Field, garden.
[7] Bravos, boasters.

couldn't help myself. She mangled her Basque words, and I believed she came from Navarre. But her eyes and her mouth and her skin were enough to prove she was a gipsy. I was mad, I paid no more attention to anything, I thought to myself that if the Spaniards had dared to speak evil of my country, I would have slashed their faces just as she had slashed her comrade's. In short, I was like a drunken man, I was beginning to say foolish things, and I was very near doing them.

"'If I were to give you a push and you tumbled down, good fellow-countryman,' she began again in Basque, 'those two Castilian recruits wouldn't be able to keep me back.'

"Faith, I forgot my orders, I forgot everything, and I said to her, 'Well, then, my friend, girl of my country, try it, and may our Lady of the Mountain help you through.'

"Just at that moment we were passing one of the many narrow lanes one sees in Seville. All at once Carmen turned and struck me in the chest with her fist. I tumbled backward, purposely. With a bound she sprang over me, and ran off, showing us a pair of legs! People talk about a pair of Basque legs! but hers were far better—as fleet as they were well-turned. As for me, I picked myself up at once, but I stuck out my lance[8] crossways and barred the street, so that

---

[8]All Spanish cavalry soldiers carry lances.

my comrades were checked at the very first moment
of pursuit. Then I started to run myself, and they
after me—but how were we to catch her? There was
no fear of that, what with our spurs, our swords, and
our lances.

"In less time than I have taken to tell you the story
the prisoner had disappeared. And besides, every
gossip in the quarter covered her flight, poked scorn
at us, and pointed us in the wrong direction. After
a good deal of marching and countermarching, we
had to go back to the guard-room without a receipt
from the governor of the jail.

"To avoid punishment, my men made known that
Carmen had spoken to me in Basque; and to tell
the truth, it did not seem very natural that a blow
from such a little creature should have so easily over-
thrown a strong fellow like me. The whole thing
looked suspicious, or, at all events, not over-clear.
When I came off guard I lost my corporal's stripes,
and was condemned to a month's imprisonment. It
was the first time I had been punished since I had
been in the service. Farewell, now, to the sergeant's
stripes, on which I had reckoned so surely!

"The first days in prison were very dreary. When I
enlisted I had fancied I was sure to become an officer,
at all events. Two of my compatriots, Longa and
Mina, are captains-general, after all. Chapalangarra
was a colonel, and I have played tennis a score of

times with his brother, who was just a needy fellow like myself. 'Now,' I kept crying to myself, 'all the time you served without being punished has been lost. Now you have a bad mark against your name, and to get yourself back into the officers' good graces you'll have to work ten times as hard as when you joined as a recruit.' And why have I got myself punished? For the sake of a gipsy hussy, who made game of me, and who at this moment is busy thieving in some corner of the town. Yet I couldn't help thinking about her. Will you believe it, sir, those silk stockings of hers with the holes in them, of which she had given me such a full view as she took to her heels, were always before my eyes? I used to look through the barred windows of the jail into the street, and among all the women who passed I never could see one to compare with that minx of a girl—and then, in spite of myself, I used to smell the acacia blossom she had thrown at me, and which, dry as it was, still kept its sweet scent. If there are such things as witches, that girl certainly was one.

"One day the jailer came in, and gave me an Alcala roll.[9]

"'Look here,' said he, 'this is what your cousin has sent you.'

"I took the loaf, very much astonished, for I had

---

[9]Alcala de los Panaderos, a village two leagues from Seville, where the most delicious rolls are made. They are said to owe their quality to the water of the place, and great quantities of them are brought to Seville every day.

no cousin in Seville. It may be a mistake, thought I, as I looked at the roll, but it was so appetizing and smelt so good, that I made up my mind to eat it, without troubling my head as to whence it came, or for whom it was really intended.

"When I tried to cut it, my knife struck on something hard. I looked, and found a little English file, which had been slipped into the dough before the roll had been baked. The roll also contained a gold piece of two piastres. Then I had no further doubt—it was a present from Carmen. To people of her blood, liberty is everything, and they would set a town on fire to save themselves one day in prison. The girl was artful, indeed, and armed with that roll, I might have snapped my fingers at the jailers. In one hour, with that little file, I could have sawn through the thickest bar, and with the gold coin I could have exchanged my soldier's cloak for civilian garb at the nearest shop. You may fancy that a man who has often taken the eaglets out of their nests in our cliff would have found no difficulty in getting down to the street out of a window less than thirty feet above it. But I didn't choose to escape. I still had a soldier's code of honour, and desertion appeared to me in the light of a heinous crime. Yet this proof of remembrance touched me. When a man is in prison he likes to think he has a friend outside who takes an interest in him. The gold coin did rather offend me; I should have very much liked to return it; but where was I to find my creditor? That did not seem a very easy task.

"After the ceremony of my degradation I had fancied my sufferings were over, but I had another humiliation before me. That came when I left prison, and was told off for duty, and put on sentry, as a private soldier. You can not conceive what a proud man endures at such a moment. I believe I would have just as soon been shot dead—then I should have marched alone at the head of my platoon, at all events; I should have felt I was somebody, with the eyes of others fixed upon me.

"I was posted as sentry on the door of the colonel's house. The colonel was a young man, rich, good-natured, fond of amusing himself. All the young officers were there, and many civilians as well, besides ladies—actresses, as it was said. For my part, it seemed to me as if the whole town had agreed to meet at that door, in order to stare at me. Then up drove the colonel's carriage, with his valet on the box. And who should I see get out of it, but the gipsy girl! She was dressed up, this time, to the eyes, togged out in golden ribbons—a spangled gown, blue shoes, all spangled too, flowers and gold lace all over her. In her hand she carried a tambourine. With her there were two other gipsy women, one young and one old. They always have one old woman who goes with them, and then an old man with a guitar, a gipsy too, to play alone, and also for their dances. You must know these gipsy girls are often sent for to private houses, to dance their special dance, the *Romalis*, and often, too, for quite other purposes.

"Carmen recognised me, and we exchanged glances. I don't know why, but at that moment I should have liked to have been a hundred feet beneath the ground.

"'*Agur laguna*,'[10] said she. 'Oficial mio! You keep guard like a recruit,' and before I could find a word in answer, she was inside the house.

"The whole party was assembled in the *patio*, and in spite of the crowd I could see nearly everything that went on through the lattice.[11] I could hear the castanets and the tambourine, the laughter and applause. Sometimes I caught a glimpse of her head as she bounded upward with her tambourine. Then I could hear the officers saying many things to her which brought the blood to my face. As to her answers, I knew nothing of them. It was on that day, I think, that I began to love her in earnest—for three or four times I was tempted to rush into the *patio*, and drive my sword into the bodies of all the coxcombs who were making love to her. My torture

---

[10] Good-day, comrade!

[11] In most of the houses in Seville there is an inner court surrounded by an arched portico. This is used as a sitting-room in summer. Over the court is stretched a piece of tent cloth, which is watered during the day and removed at night. The street door is almost always left open, and the passage leading to the court (zaguan) is closed by an iron lattice of very elegant workmanship.

lasted a full hour; then the gipsies came out, and the carriage took them away. As she passed me by, Carmen looked at me with those eyes you know, and said to me very low, 'Comrade, people who are fond of good *fritata* come to eat it at Lillas Pastia's at Triana!'

"Then, light as a kid, she stepped into the carriage, the coachman whipped up his mules, and the whole merry party departed, whither I know not.

"You may fancy that the moment I was off guard I went to Triana; but first of all I got myself shaved and brushed myself up as if I had been going on parade. She was living with Lillas Pastia, an old fried-fish seller, a gipsy, as black as a Moor, to whose house a great many civilians resorted to eat *fritata*, especially, I think, because Carmen had taken up her quarters there.

"'Lillas,' she said, as soon as she saw me. 'I'm not going to work any more to-day. To-morrow will be a day, too.[12] Come, fellow-countryman, let us go for a walk!'

"She pulled her mantilla across her nose, and there we were in the street, without my knowing in the least whither I was bound.

"'Señorita,' said I, 'I think I have to thank you for a present I had while I was in prison. I've eaten the bread; the file will do for sharpening my lance, and I keep it in remembrance of you. But as for the money,

---

[12] Mañana sera otro dia.—A Spanish proverb.

here it is.'

"'Why, he's kept the money!' she exclaimed, bursting out laughing. 'But, after all, that's all the better—for I'm decidedly hard up! What matter! The dog that runs never starves![13] Come, let's spend it all! You shall treat.'

"We had turned back toward Seville. At the entrance of the *Calle de la Serpiente* she bought a dozen oranges, which she made me put into my handkerchief. A little farther on she bought a roll, a sausage, and a bottle of manzanilla. Then, last of all, she turned into a confectioner's shop. There she threw the gold coin I had returned to her on the counter, with another she had in her pocket, and some small silver, and then she asked me for all the money I had. All I possessed was one peseta and a few cuartos, which I handed over to her, very much ashamed of not having more. I thought she would have carried away the whole shop. She took everything that was best and dearest, *yemas*,[14] *turon*,[15] preserved fruits—as long as the money lasted. And all these, too, I had to carry in paper bags. Perhaps you know the *Calle del Candilejo*, where there is a head of Don Pedro the Avenger.[16] That head ought to have given me pause.

[13]Chuquel sos pirela, cocal terela. "The dog that runs finds a bone."—Gipsy proverb.

[14]Sugared yolks of eggs.

[15]A sort of nougat.

[16]This king, Don Pedro, whom we call "the Cruel," and whom Queen Isabella, the Catholic, never called anything but "the Avenger," was fond of walking about the streets of Seville at night

We stopped at an old house in that street. She passed into the entry, and knocked at a door on the ground floor. It was opened by a gipsy, a thorough-paced servant of the devil. Carmen said a few words to her in Romany. At first the old hag grumbled. To smooth her down Carmen gave her a couple of oranges and a handful of sugar-plums, and let her have a taste of wine. Then she hung her cloak on her back, and led her to the door, which she fastened with a wooden bar. As soon as we were alone she began to laugh and caper like a lunatic, singing out, 'You are my *rom*, I'm

---

in search of adventures, like the Caliph Haroun al Raschid. One night, in a lonely street, he quarrelled with a man who was singing a serenade. There was a fight, and the king killed the amorous caballero. At the clashing of their swords, an old woman put her head out of the window and lighted up the scene with a tiny lamp (candilejo) which she held in her hand. My readers must be informed that King Don Pedro, though nimble and muscular, suffered from one strange fault in his physical conformation. Whenever he walked his knees cracked loudly. By this cracking the old woman easily recognised him.

The next day the veintiquatro in charge came to make his report to the king. "Sir, a duel was fought last night in such a street—one of the combatants is dead." "Have you found the murderer?" "Yes, sir." "Why has he not been punished already?" "Sir, I await your orders!" "Carry out the law." Now the king had just published a decree that every duellist was to have his head cut off, and that head was to be set up on the scene of the fight. The veintiquatro got out of the difficulty like a clever man. He had the head sawed off a statue of the king, and set that up in a niche in the middle of the street in which the murder had taken place. The king and all the Sevillians thought this a very good joke. The street took its name from the lamp held by the old woman, the only witness of the incident. The above is the popular tradition. Zuniga tells the story somewhat differently. However that may be, a street called Calle del Candilejo still exists in Seville, and in that street there is a bust which is said to be a portrait of Don Pedro. This bust, unfortunately, is a modern production. During the seventeenth century the old one had become very much defaced, and the municipality had it replaced by that now to be seen.

your *romi*.[17]

"There I stood in the middle of the room, laden with all her purchases, and not knowing where I was to put them down. She tumbled them all onto the floor, and threw her arms round my neck, saying:

"'I pay my debts, I pay my debts! That's the law of the *Cales*.'[18]

"Ah, sir, that day! that day! When I think of it I forget what to-morrow must bring me!"

For a moment the bandit held his peace, then, when he had relighted his cigar, he began afresh.

"We spent the whole day together, eating, drinking, and so forth. When she had stuffed herself with sugar-plums, like any child of six years old, she thrust them by handfuls into the old woman's water-jar. 'That'll make sherbet for her,' she said. She smashed the *yemas* by throwing them against the walls. 'They'll keep the flies from bothering us.' There was no prank or wild frolic she didn't indulge in. I told her I should have liked to see her dance, only there were no castanets to be had. Instantly she seized the old woman's only earthenware plate, smashed it up, and there she was dancing the *Romalis*, and making the bits of broken crockery rattle as well as if they had been ebony and ivory castanets. That girl was good company, I can tell you! Evening fell, and I heard the drums

---

[17]Rom, husband. Romi, wife.
[18]Calo, feminine calli, plural cales. Literally "black," the name the gipsies apply to themselves in their own language.

beating tattoo.

"'I must get back to quarters for roll-call,' I said.

"'To quarters!' she answered, with a look of scorn. 'Are you a negro slave, to let yourself be driven with a ramrod like that! You are as silly as a canary bird. Your dress suits your nature.[19] Pshaw! you've no more heart than a chicken.'

"I stayed on, making up my mind to the inevitable guard-room. The next morning the first suggestion of parting came from her.

"'Hark ye, Joseito,' she said. 'Have I paid you? By our law, I owed you nothing, because you're a *payllo*. But you're a good-looking fellow, and I took a fancy to you. Now we're quits. Good-day!'

"I asked her when I should see her again.

"'When you're less of a simpleton,' she retorted, with a laugh. Then, in a more serious tone, 'Do you know, my son, I really believe I love you a little; but that can't last! The dog and the wolf can't agree for long. Perhaps if you turned gipsy, I might care to be your *romi*. But that's all nonsense, such things aren't possible. Pshaw! my boy. Believe me, you're well out of it. You've come across the devil—he isn't always black—and you've not had your neck wrung. I wear a woollen suit, but I'm no sheep.[20] Go and

---

[19] Spanish dragoons wear a yellow uniform.
[20] Me dicas vriarda de jorpoy, bus ne sino braco.—A gipsy proverb.

burn a candle to your *majari*,[21] she deserves it well. Come, good-by once more. Don't think any more about *La Carmencita*, or she'll end by making you marry a widow with wooden legs.'[22]

"As she spoke, she drew back the bar that closed the door, and once we were out in the street she wrapped her mantilla about her, and turned on her heel.

"She spoke the truth. I should have done far better never to think of her again. But after that day in the *Calle del Candilejo* I couldn't think of anything else. All day long I used to walk about, hoping I might meet her. I sought news of her from the old hag, and from the fried-fish seller. They both told me she had gone away to *Laloro*, which is their name for Portugal. They probably said it by Carmen's orders, but I soon found out they were lying. Some weeks after my day in the *Calle del Candilejo* I was on duty at one of the town gates. A little way from the gate there was a breach in the wall. The masons were working at it in the daytime, and at night a sentinel was posted on it, to prevent smugglers from getting in. All through one day I saw Lillas Pastia going backward and forward near the guard-room, and talking to some of my comrades. They all knew him well, and his fried-fish and fritters even better. He came up to me, and

---

[21] The Saint, the Holy Virgin.
[22] The gallows, which is the widow of the last man hanged upon it.

asked if I had any news of Carmen.

"'No,' said I.

"'Well,' said he, 'you'll soon hear of her, old fellow.'

"He was not mistaken. That night I was posted to guard the breach in the wall. As soon as the sergeant had disappeared I saw a woman coming toward me. My heart told me it was Carmen. Still I shouted:

"'Keep off! Nobody can pass here!'

"'Now, don't be spiteful,' she said, making herself known to me.

"'What! you here, Carmen?'

"'Yes, *mi payllo*. Let us say few words, but wise ones. Would you like to earn a douro? Some people will be coming with bundles. Let them alone.'

"'No,' said I, 'I must not allow them through. These are my orders.'

"'Orders! orders! You didn't think about orders in the *Calle del Candilejo*!'

"'Ah!' I cried, quite maddened by the very thought of that night. 'It was well worth while to forget my orders for that! But I won't have any smuggler's money!'

"'Well, if you won't have money, shall we go and dine together at old Dorotea's?'

"'No,' said I, half choked by the effort it cost me. 'No, I can't.'

"'Very good! If you make so many difficulties, I know to whom I can go. I'll ask your officer if he'll come with me to Dorotea's. He looks good-natured, and he'll post a sentry who'll only see what he had better see. Good-bye, canary-bird! I shall have a good laugh the day the order comes out to hang you!'

"I was weak enough to call her back, and I promised to let the whole of gipsydom pass in, if that were necessary, so that I secured the only reward I longed for. She instantly swore she would keep her word faithfully the very next day, and ran off to summon her friends, who were close by. There were five of them, of whom Pastia was one, all well loaded with English goods. Carmen kept watch for them. She was to warn them with her castanets the instant she caught sight of the patrol. But there was no necessity for that. The smugglers finished their job in a moment.

"The next day I went to the *Calle del Candilejo*. Carmen kept me waiting, and when she came, she was in rather a bad temper.

"'I don't like people who have to be pressed,' she said. 'You did me a much greater service the first time, without knowing you'd gain anything by it. Yesterday you bargained with me. I don't know why I've come, for I don't care for you any more. Here, be off with you. Here's a douro for your trouble.'

"I very nearly threw the coin at her head, and I had to make a violent effort to prevent myself from actually beating her. After we had wrangled for an hour I went off in a fury. For some time I wandered about the town, walking hither and thither like a madman. At last I went into a church, and getting into the darkest corner I could find, I cried hot tears. All at once I heard a voice.

"'A dragoon in tears. I'll make a philter of them!'

"I looked up. There was Carmen in front of me.

"'Well, *mi payllo*, are you still angry with me?' she said. 'I must care for you in spite of myself, for since you left me I don't know what has been the matter with me. Look you, it is I who ask you to come to the *Calle del Candilejo*, now!'

"So we made it up: but Carmen's temper was like the weather in our country. The storm is never so close, in our mountains, as when the sun is at its brightest. She had promised to meet me again at Dorotea's, but she didn't come.

"And Dorotea began telling me again that she had gone off to Portugal about some gipsy business.

"As experience had already taught me how much of that I was to believe, I went about looking for Carmen wherever I thought she might be, and twenty times in every day I walked through the *Calle del Candilejo*. One evening I was with Dorotea, whom I had almost tamed by giving her a glass of anisette now and then, when Carmen walked in, followed by a young man, a lieutenant in our regiment.

"'Get away at once,' she said to me in Basque. I stood there, dumfounded, my heart full of rage.

"'What are you doing here?' said the lieutenant to me. 'Take yourself off—get out of this.'

"I couldn't move a step. I felt paralyzed. The officer grew angry, and seeing I did not go out, and had not even taken off my forage cap, he caught me by the collar and shook me roughly. I don't know what I said to him. He drew his sword, and I unsheathed mine. The old woman caught hold of my arm, and the lieutenant gave me a wound on the forehead, of which I still bear the scar. I made a step backward, and with one jerk of my elbow I threw old Dorotea down. Then, as the lieutenant still pressed me, I turned the point of my sword against his body and he ran upon it. Then Carmen put out the lamp and told Dorotea, in her own language, to take to flight. I fled into the street myself, and began running along, I knew not whither. It seemed to me that some one was following me. When I came to myself I discovered that Carmen had never left me.

"'Great stupid of a canary-bird!' she said, 'you never make anything but blunders. And, indeed, you know I told you I should bring you bad luck. But come, there's a cure for everything when you have a Fleming from Rome[23] for your love. Begin by rolling

---

[23] Flamenco de Roma, a slang term for the gipsies. Roma does not stand for the Eternal City, but for the nation of the romi, or the married folk—a name applied by the gipsies to themselves. The

this handkerchief round your head, and throw me over that belt of yours. Wait for me in this alley—I'll be back in two minutes.

"She disappeared, and soon came back bringing me a striped cloak which she had gone to fetch, I knew not whence. She made me take off my uniform, and put on the cloak over my shirt. Thus dressed, and with the wound on my head bound round with the handkerchief, I was tolerably like a Valencian peasant, many of whom come to Seville to sell a drink they make out of '*chufas*.'[24] Then she took me to a house very much like Dorotea's, at the bottom of a little lane. Here she and another gipsy woman washed and dressed my wounds, better than any army surgeon could have done, gave me something, I know not what, to drink, and finally made me lie down on a mattress, on which I went to sleep.

"Probably the woman had mixed one of the soporific drugs of which they know the secret in my drink, for I did not wake up till very late the next day. I was rather feverish, and had a violent headache. It was some time before the memory of the terrible scene in which I had taken part on the previous night came back to me. After having dressed my wound, Carmen and her friend, squatting on their heels beside my mattress, exchanged a few words of '*chipe*

---

first gipsies seen in Spain probably came from the Low Countries, hence their name of Flemings.

[24] A bulbous root, out of which rather a pleasant beverage is manufactured.

calli,' which appeared to me to be something in the nature of a medical consultation. Then they both of them assured me that I should soon be cured, but that I must get out of Seville at the earliest possible moment, for that, if I was caught there, I should most undoubtedly be shot.

"'My boy,' said Carmen to me, 'you'll have to do something. Now that the king won't give you either rice or haddock[25] you'll have to think of earning your livelihood. You're too stupid for stealing *a paste-sas*.[26] But you are brave and active. If you have the pluck, take yourself off to the coast and turn smuggler. Haven't I promised to get you hanged? That's better than being shot, and besides, if you set about it properly, you'll live like a prince as long as the *minons*[27] and the coast-guard don't lay their hands on your collar.'

"In this attractive guise did this fiend of a girl describe the new career she was suggesting to me,—the only one, indeed, remaining, now I had incurred the penalty of death. Shall I confess it, sir? She persuaded me without much difficulty. This wild and dangerous life, it seemed to me, would bind her and me more closely together. In future, I thought, I should be able to make sure of her love.

"I had often heard talk of certain smugglers who

---

[25]The ordinary food of a Spanish soldier.
[26]Ustilar a pastesas, to steal cleverly, to purloin without violence.
[27]A sort of volunteer corps.

travelled about Andalusia, each riding a good horse, with his mistress behind him and his blunderbuss in his fist. Already I saw myself trotting up and down the world, with a pretty gipsy behind me. When I mentioned that notion to her, she laughed till she had to hold her sides, and vowed there was nothing in the world so delightful as a night spent camping in the open air, when each *rom* retired with his *romi* beneath their little tent, made of three hoops with a blanket thrown across them.

"'If I take to the mountains,' said I to her, 'I shall be sure of you. There'll be no lieutenant there to go shares with me.'

"'Ha! ha! you're jealous!' she retorted, 'so much the worse for you. How can you be such a fool as that? Don't you see I must love you, because I have never asked you for money?'

"When she said that sort to thing I could have strangled her.

"To shorten the story, sir, Carmen procured me civilian clothes, disguised in which I got out of Seville without being recognised. I went to Jerez, with a letter from Pastia to a dealer in anisette whose house was the smugglers' meeting-place. I was introduced to them, and their leader, surnamed *El Dancaire*, enrolled me in his gang. We started for Gaucin, where I found Carmen, who had told me she would meet me there. In all these expeditions she acted as spy for our gang, and she was the best that ever was seen. She had now just returned from Gibraltar, and had already arranged with the captain of a ship for a cargo of English goods which we were to receive on the coast. We went to meet it near Estepona. We hid part in the mountains, and laden with the rest, we proceeded to Ronda. Carmen had gone there before us. It was she again who warned us when we had better enter the town. This first journey, and several subsequent ones, turned out well. I found the smuggler's life pleasanter than a soldier's: I could give presents to Carmen, I had money, and I had a mistress. I felt little or no remorse, for, as the gipsies say, 'The happy man never longs to scratch his itch.' We were made welcome everywhere, my comrades treated me well, and even showed me a certain respect. The reason of this was that I had killed my man, and that some of them had no exploit of that description on their conscience. But what I valued most in my new life was that I often saw Carmen. She showed me more affection than ever; nevertheless, she would never admit, before my comrades, that she was my mistress, and she had even made me swear all sorts of oaths that I would not say anything about her to them. I was so weak in that creature's hands, that I obeyed all her whims. And besides, this was the first time she had revealed herself as possessing any of the reserve of a well-conducted woman, and I was simple enough to believe she had really cast off her former habits.

"Our gang, which consisted of eight or ten men, was hardly ever together except at decisive moments, and we were usually scattered by twos and threes about the towns and villages. Each one of us pretended to have some trade. One was a tinker, another was a groom; I was supposed to peddle haberdashery, but I hardly ever showed myself in large places, on account of my unlucky business at Seville. One day, or rather one night, we were to meet below Veger. *El Dancaire* and I got there before the others.

"'We shall soon have a new comrade,' said he. 'Carmen has just managed one of her best tricks. She has contrived the escape of her *rom*, who was in the *presidio* at Tarifa.'

"I was already beginning to understand the gipsy language, which nearly all my comrades spoke, and this word *rom* startled me.

"'What! her husband? Is she married, then?' said I to the captain.

"'Yes!' he replied, 'married to Garcia *el Tuerto*[28]— as cunning a gipsy as she is herself. The poor fellow has been at the galleys. Carmen has wheedled the surgeon of the *presidio* to such good purpose that she has managed to get her *rom* out of prison. Faith! that girl's worth her weight in gold. For two years she has

---

[28]One-eyed man.

been trying to contrive his escape, but she could do nothing until the authorities took it into their heads to change the surgeon. She soon managed to come to an understanding with this new one.'

"You may imagine how pleasant this news was for me. I soon saw Garcia *el Tuerto*. He was the very ugliest brute that was ever nursed in gipsydom. His skin was black, his soul was blacker, and he was altogether the most thorough-paced ruffian I ever came across in my life. Carmen arrived with him, and when she called him her *rom* in my presence, you should have seen the eyes she made at me, and the faces she pulled whenever Garcia turned his head away.

"I was disgusted, and never spoke a word to her all night. The next morning we had made up our packs, and had already started, when we became aware that we had a dozen horsemen on our heels. The braggart Andalusians, who had been boasting they would murder every one who came near them, cut a pitiful figure at once. There was a general rout. *El Dancaire*, Garcia, a good-looking fellow from Ecija, who was called *El Remendado*, and Carmen herself, kept their wits about them. The rest forsook the mules and took to the gorges, where the horses could not follow them. There was no hope of saving the mules, so we hastily unstrapped the best part of our booty, and taking it on our shoulders, we tried to escape through

the rocks down the steepest of the slopes. We threw
our packs down in front of us and followed them as
best we could, slipping along on our heels. Meanwhile the enemy fired at us. It was the first time I had
ever heard bullets whistling around me and I didn't
mind it very much. When there's a woman looking on, there's no particular merit in snapping one's
fingers at death. We all escaped except the poor *Remendado*, who received a bullet wound in the loins. I
threw away my pack and tried to lift him up.

"'Idiot!' shouted Garcia, 'what do we want with
offal! Finish him off, and don't lose the cotton stockings!'

"'Drop him!' cried Carmen.

"I was so exhausted that I was obliged to lay him
down for a moment under a rock. Garcia came up,
and fired his blunderbuss full into his face. 'He'd be
a clever fellow who recognised him now!' said he, as
he looked at the face, cut to pieces by a dozen slugs.

"There, sir; that's the delightful sort of life I've led!
That night we found ourselves in a thicket, worn out
with fatigue, with nothing to eat, and ruined by the
loss of our mules. What do you think that devil Garcia did? He pulled a pack of cards out of his pocket
and began playing games with *El Dancaire* by the
light of a fire they kindled. Meanwhile I was lying
down, staring at the stars, thinking of *El Remendado*,
and telling myself I would just as lief be in his place.

Carmen was squatting down near me, and every now and then she would rattle her castanets and hum a tune. Then, drawing close to me, as if she would have whispered in my ear, she kissed me two or three times over almost against my will.

"'You are a devil,' said I to her.

"'Yes,' she replied.

"After a few hours' rest, she departed to Gaucin, and the next morning a little goatherd brought us some food. We stayed there all that day, and in the evening we moved close to Gaucin. We were expecting news from Carmen, but none came. After daylight broke we saw a muleteer attending a well-dressed woman with a parasol, and a little girl who seemed to be her servant. Said Garcia, 'There go two mules and two women whom St. Nicholas has sent us. I would rather have had four mules, but no matter. I'll do the best I can with these.'

"He took his blunderbuss, and went down the pathway, hiding himself among the brushwood.

"We followed him, *El Dancaire* and I keeping a little way behind. As soon as the woman saw us, instead of being frightened—and our dress would have been enough to frighten any one—she burst into a fit of loud laughter. 'Ah! the *lillipendi*! They take me for an *erani*!'[29]

"It was Carmen, but so well disguised that if she

---

[29]"The idiots, they take me for a smart lady!"

had spoken any other language I should never have recognised her. She sprang off her mule, and talked some time in an undertone with *El Dancaire* and Garcia. Then she said to me:

"'Canary-bird, we shall meet again before you're hanged. I'm off to Gibraltar on gipsy business—you'll soon have news of me.'

"We parted, after she had told us of a place where we should find shelter for some days. That girl was the providence of our gang. We soon received some money sent by her, and a piece of news which was still more useful to us—to the effect that on a certain day two English lords would travel from Gibraltar to Granada by a road she mentioned. This was a word to the wise. They had plenty of good guineas. Garcia would have killed them, but *El Dancaire* and I objected. All we took from them, besides their shirts, which we greatly needed, was their money and their watches.

"Sir, a man may turn rogue in sheer thoughtlessness. You lose your head over a pretty girl, you fight another man about her, there is a catastrophe, you have to take to the mountains, and you turn from a smuggler into a robber before you have time to think about it. After this matter of the English lords, we concluded that the neighbourhood of Gibraltar would not be healthy for us, and we plunged into the *Sierra de Ronda*. You once mentioned Jose-Maria to me. Well, it was there I made acquaintance with him. He always took his mistress with him on his expeditions. She was a pretty girl, quiet, modest, well-mannered, you never heard a vulgar word from her, and she was quite devoted to him. He, on his side, led her a very unhappy life. He was always running after other women, he ill-treated her, and then sometimes he would take it into his head to be jealous. One day he slashed her with a knife. Well, she only doted on him the more! That's the way with women, and especially with Andalusians. This girl was proud of the scar on her arm, and would display it as though it were the most beautiful thing in the world. And then Jose-Maria was the worst of comrades in the bargain. In one expedition we made with him, he managed so that he kept all the profits, and we had all the trouble and the blows. But I must go back to my story. We had no sign at all from Carmen. *El Dancaire* said: 'One of us will have to go to Gibraltar to get news of her. She must have planned some business. I'd go at once, only I'm too well known at Gibraltar.' *El Tuerto* said:

"'I'm well known there too. I've played so many tricks on the crayfish[30]—and as I've only one eye, it is not overeasy for me to disguise myself.'

"'Then I suppose I must go,' said I, delighted at the very idea of seeing Carmen again. 'Well, how am

---

[30]Name applied by the Spanish populace to the British soldiers, on account of the colour of their uniform.

I to set about it?'

"The others answered:

"'You must either go by sea, or you must get through by San Rocco, whichever you like the best; once you are in Gibraltar, inquire in the port where a chocolate-seller called *La Rollona* lives. When you've found her, she'll tell you everything that's happening.'

"It was settled that we were all to start for the Sierra, that I was to leave my two companions there, and take my way to Gibraltar, in the character of a fruit-seller. At Ronda one of our men procured me a passport; at Gaucin I was provided with a donkey. I loaded it with oranges and melons, and started forth. When I reached Gibraltar I found that many people knew *La Rollona*, but that she was either dead or had gone *ad finibus terroe*,[31] and, to my mind, her disappearance explained the failure of our correspondence with Carmen. I stabled my donkey, and began to move about the town, carrying my oranges as though to sell them, but in reality looking to see whether I could not come across any face I knew. The place is full of ragamuffins from every country in the world, and it really is like the Tower of Babel, for you can't go ten paces along a street without hearing as many languages. I did see some gipsies, but I hardly dared confide in them. I was taking stock of them,

---

[31]To the galleys, or else to all the devils in hell.

and they were taking stock of me. We had mutually guessed each other to be rogues, but the important thing for us was to know whether we belonged to the same gang. After having spent two days in fruitless wanderings, and having found out nothing either as to *La Rollona* or as to Carmen, I was thinking I would go back to my comrades as soon as I had made a few purchases, when, toward sunset, as I was walking along a street, I heard a woman's voice from a window say, 'Orange-seller!'

"I looked up, and on a balcony I saw Carmen looking out, beside a scarlet-coated officer with gold epaulettes, curly hair, and all the appearance of a rich *milord*. As for her, she was magnificently dressed, a shawl hung on her shoulders, she'd a gold comb in her hair, everything she wore was of silk; and the cunning little wretch, not a bit altered, was laughing till she held her sides.

"The Englishman shouted to me in mangled Spanish to come upstairs, as the lady wanted some oranges, and Carmen said to me in Basque:

"'Come up, and don't look astonished at anything!'

"Indeed, nothing that she did ought ever to have astonished me. I don't know whether I was most happy or wretched at seeing her again. At the door of the house there was a tall English servant with a powdered head, who ushered me into a splendid drawing-room. Instantly Carmen said to me in Basque, 'You don't know one word of Spanish, and you don't know me.' Then turning to the Englishman, she added:

"'I told you so. I saw at once he was a Basque. Now you'll hear what a queer language he speaks. Doesn't he look silly? He's like a cat that's been caught in the larder!'

"'And you,' said I to her in my own language, 'you look like an impudent jade—and I've a good mind to scar your face here and now, before your spark.'

"'My spark!' said she. 'Why, you've guessed that all alone! Are you jealous of this idiot? You're even sillier than you were before our evening in the *Calle del Candilejo*! Don't you see, fool, that at this moment I'm doing gipsy business, and doing it in the most brilliant manner? This house belongs to me—the guineas of that crayfish will belong to me! I lead him by the nose, and I'll lead him to a place that he'll never get out of!'

"'And if I catch you doing any gipsy business in this style again, I'll see to it that you never do any again!' said I.

"'Ah! upon my word! Are you my *rom*, pray that you give me orders? If *El Tuerto* is pleased, what have you to do with it? Oughtn't you to be very happy that you are the only man who can call himself my *min-chorro*?'[32]

"'What does he say?' inquired the Englishman.

---

[32] My "lover," or rather my "fancy."

67

"'He says he's thirsty, and would like a drink,' answered Carmen, and she threw herself back upon a sofa, screaming with laughter at her own translation.

"When that girl begins to laugh, sir, it was hopeless for anybody to try and talk sense. Everybody laughed with her. The big Englishman began to laugh too, like the idiot he was, and ordered the servant to bring me something to drink.

"While I was drinking she said to me:

"'Do you see that ring he has on his finger? If you like I'll give it to you.'

"And I answered:

"'I would give one of my fingers to have your *milord* out on the mountains, and each of us with a *maquila* in his fist.'

"'*Maquila*, what does that mean?' asked the Englishman.

"'Maquila,' said Carmen, still laughing, 'means an orange. Isn't it a queer word for an orange? He says he'd like you to eat *maquila*.'

"'Does he?' said the Englishman. 'Very well, bring more *maquila* to-morrow.'

"While we were talking a servant came in and said dinner was ready. Then the Englishman stood up, gave me a piastre, and offered his arm to Carmen, as if she couldn't have walked alone. Carmen, who was still laughing, said to me:

"'My boy, I can't ask you to dinner. But to-morrow,

as soon as you hear the drums beat for parade, come here with your oranges. You'll find a better furnished room than the one in the *Calle del Candilejo*, and you'll see whether I am still your *Carmencita*. Then afterwards we'll talk about gipsy business.'

"I gave her no answer—even when I was in the street I could hear the Englishman shouting, 'Bring more *maquila* to-morrow,' and Carmen's peals of laughter.

"I went out, not knowing what I should do; I hardly slept, and next morning I was so enraged with the treacherous creature that I made up my mind to leave Gibraltar without seeing her again. But the moment the drums began to roll, my courage failed me. I took up my net full of oranges, and hurried off to Carmen's house. Her window-shutters had been pulled apart a little, and I saw her great dark eyes watching for me. The powdered servant showed me in at once. Carmen sent him out with a message, and as soon as we were alone she burst into one of her fits of crocodile laughter and threw her arms around my neck. Never had I seen her look so beautiful. She was dressed out like a queen, and scented; she had silken furniture, embroidered curtains—and I togged out like the thief I was!

"'*Minchorro*,' said Carmen, 'I've a good mind to smash up everything here, set fire to the house, and take myself off to the mountains.' And then she would fondle me, and then she would laugh, and she danced about and tore up her fripperies. Never did monkey gambol nor make such faces, nor play such wild tricks, as she did that day. When she had recovered her gravity—

"'Hark!' she said, 'this is gipsy business. I mean him to take me to Ronda, where I have a sister who is a nun' (here she shrieked with laughter again). 'We shall pass by a particular spot which I shall make known to you. Then you must fall upon him and strip him to the skin. Your best plan would be to do for him, but,' she added, with a certain fiendish smile of hers, which no one who saw it ever had any desire to imitate, 'do you know what you had better do? Let *El Tuerto* come up in front of you. You keep a little behind. The crayfish is brave, and skilful too, and he has good pistols. Do you understand?'

"And she broke off with another fit of laughter that made me shiver.

"'No,' said I, 'I hate Garcia, but he's my comrade. Some day, maybe, I'll rid you of him, but we'll settle our account after the fashion of my country. It's only chance that has made me a gipsy, and in certain things I shall always be a thorough Navarrese,[33] as the proverb says.

"'You're a fool,' she rejoined, 'a simpleton, a regular *payllo*. You're just like the dwarf who thinks him-

---

[33]Navarro fino.

self tall because he can spit a long way.[34] You don't love me! Be off with you!'

"Whenever she said to me 'Be off with you," I couldn't go away. I promised I would start back to my comrades and wait the arrival of the Englishman. She, on her side, promised she would be ill until she left Gibraltar for Ronda.

"I remained at Gibraltar two days longer. She had the boldness to disguise herself and come and see me at the inn. I departed, I had a plan of my own. I went back to our meeting-place with the information as to the spot and the hour at which the Englishman and Carmen were to pass by. I found *El Dancaire* and Garcia waiting for me. We spent the night in a wood, beside a fire made of pine-cones that blazed splendidly. I suggested to Garcia that we should play cards, and he agreed. In the second game I told him he was cheating; he began to laugh; I threw the cards in his face. He tried to get at his blunderbuss. I set my foot on it, and said, 'They say you can use a knife as well as the best ruffian in Malaga; will you try it with me?' *El Dancaire* tried to part us. I had given Garcia one or two cuffs, his rage had given him courage, he drew his knife, and I drew mine. We both of us told *El Dancaire* he must leave us alone, and let us fight it out. He saw there was no means of stopping us, so he stood on one side. Garcia was already bent double,

---

[34]Or esorjle de or marsichisle, sin chisnar lachinguel. "The promise of a dwarf is that he will spit a long way."—A gipsy proverb.

like a cat ready to spring upon a mouse. He held his hat in his left hand to parry with, and his knife in front of him—that's their Andalusian guard. I stood up in the Navarrese fashion, with my left arm raised, my left leg forward, and my knife held straight along my right thigh. I felt I was stronger than any giant. He flew at me like an arrow. I turned round on my left foot, so that he found nothing in front of him. But I thrust him in the throat, and the knife went in so far that my hand was under his chin. I gave the blade such a twist that it broke. That was the end. The blade was carried out of the wound by a gush of blood as thick as my arm, and he fell full length on his face.

"'What have you done?' said *El Dancaire* to me.

"'Hark ye,' said I, 'we couldn't live on together. I love Carmen and I mean to be the only one. And besides, Garcia was a villain. I remember what he did to that poor *Remendado*. There are only two of us left now, but we are both good fellows. Come, will you have me for your friend, for life or death?'

"*El Dancaire* stretched out his hand. He was a man of fifty.

"'Devil take these love stories!' he cried. 'If you'd asked him for Carmen he'd have sold her to you for a piastre! There are only two of us now—how shall we manage for to-morrow?'

"'I'll manage it all alone,' I answered. 'I can snap

my fingers at the whole world now.'

"We buried Garcia, and we moved our camp two hundred paces farther on. The next morning Carmen and her Englishman came along with two muleteers and a servant. I said to *El Dancaire*:

"'I'll look after the Englishman, you frighten the others—they're not armed!'

"The Englishman was a plucky fellow. He'd have killed me if Carmen hadn't jogged his elbow.

"To put it shortly, I won Carmen back that day, and my first words were to tell her she was a widow.

"When she knew how it had all happened—

"'You'll always be a *lillipendi*,' she said. 'Garcia ought to have killed you. Your Navarrese guard is a pack of nonsense, and he has sent far more skilful men than you into the darkness. It was just that his time had come—and yours will come too.'

"'Ay, and yours too!—if you're not a faithful *romi* to me.'

"'So be it,' said she. 'I've read in the coffee grounds, more than once, that you and I were to end our lives together. Pshaw! what must be, will be!' and she rattled her castanets, as was her way when she wanted to drive away some worrying thought.

"One runs on when one is talking about one's self. I dare say all these details bore you, but I shall soon be at the end of my story. Our new life lasted for some considerable time. *El Dancaire* and I gathered a few comrades about us, who were more trustworthy than our earlier ones, and we turned our attention to smuggling. Occasionally, indeed, I must confess we stopped travellers on the highways, but never unless we were at the last extremity, and could not avoid doing so; and besides, we never ill-treated the travellers, and confined ourselves to taking their money from them.

"For some months I was very well satisfied with Carmen. She still served us in our smuggling operations, by giving us notice of any opportunity of making a good haul. She remained either at Malaga, at Cordova, or at Granada, but at a word from me she would leave everything, and come to meet me at some *venta* or even in our lonely camp. Only once— it was at Malaga—she caused me some uneasiness. I heard she had fixed her fancy upon a very rich merchant, with whom she probably proposed to play her Gibraltar trick over again. In spite of everything *El Dancaire* said to stop me, I started off, walked into Malaga in broad daylight, sought for Carmen and carried her off instantly. We had a sharp altercation.

"'Do you know,' said she, 'now that you're my *rom* for good and all, I don't care for you so much as when you were my *minchorro*! I won't be worried, and above all, I won't be ordered about. I choose to be free to do as I like. Take care you don't drive me too far; if you tire me out, I'll find some good fellow who'll serve you just as you served *El Tuerto.*'

"*El Dancaire* patched it up between us; but we had said things to each other that rankled in our hearts, and we were not as we had been before. Shortly after that we had a misfortune: the soldiers caught us, *El Dancaire* and two of my comrades were killed; two others were taken. I was sorely wounded, and, but for my good horse, I should have fallen into the soldiers' hands. Half dead with fatigue, and with a bullet in my body, I sought shelter in a wood, with my only remaining comrade. When I got off my horse I fainted away, and I thought I was going to die there in the brushwood, like a shot hare. My comrade carried me to a cave he knew of, and then he sent to fetch Carmen.

"She was at Granada, and she hurried to me at once. For a whole fortnight she never left me for a single instant. She never closed her eyes; she nursed me with a skill and care such as no woman ever showed to the man she loved most tenderly. As soon as I could stand on my feet, she conveyed me with the utmost secrecy to Granada. These gipsy women find safe shelter everywhere, and I spent more than six weeks in a house only two doors from that of the *Corregidor* who was trying to arrest me. More than once I saw him pass by, from behind the shutter. At last I recovered, but I had thought a great deal, on my bed of pain, and I had planned to change my way of life.

I suggested to Carmen that we should leave Spain, and seek an honest livelihood in the New World. She laughed in my face.

"'We were not born to plant cabbages,' she cried. 'Our fate is to live *payllos*! Listen: I've arranged a business with Nathan Ben-Joseph at Gibraltar. He has cotton stuffs that he can not get through till you come to fetch them. He knows you're alive, and reckons upon you. What would our Gibraltar correspondents say if you failed them?'

"I let myself by persuaded, and took up my vile trade once more.

"While I was hiding at Granada there were bull-fights there, to which Carmen went. When she came back she talked a great deal about a skilful *picador* of the name of Lucas. She knew the name of his horse, and how much his embroidered jacket had cost him. I paid no attention to this; but a few days later, Juanito, the only one of my comrades who was left, told me he had seen Carmen with Lucas in a shop in the Zacatin. Then I began to feel alarmed. I asked Carmen how and why she had made the *picador's* acquaintance.

"'He's a man out of whom we may be able to get something,' said she. 'A noisy stream has either water in it or pebbles. He has earned twelve hundred reals at the bull-fights. It must be one of two things: we must either have his money, or else, as he is a good rider and a plucky fellow, we can enroll him in our gang. We have lost such an one an such an one; you'll have to replace them. Take this man with you!'

"'I want neither his money nor himself,' I replied, 'and I forbid you to speak to him.'

"'Beware!' she retorted. 'If any one defies me to do a thing, it's very quickly done.'

"Luckily the *picador* departed to Malaga, and I set about passing in the Jew's cotton stuffs. This expedition gave me a great deal to do, and Carmen as well. I forgot Lucas, and perhaps she forgot him too—for the moment, at all events. It was just about that time, sir, that I met you, first at Montilla, and then afterward at Cordova. I won't talk about that last interview. You know more about it, perhaps, than I do. Carmen stole your watch from you, she wanted to have your money besides, and especially that ring I see on your finger, and which she declared to be a magic ring, the possession of which was very important to her. We had a violent quarrel, and I struck her. She turned pale and began to cry. It was the first time I had ever seen her cry, and it affected me in the most painful manner. I begged her to forgive me, but she sulked with me for a whole day, and when I started back to Montilla she wouldn't kiss me. My heart was still very sore, when, three days later, she joined me with a smiling face and as merry as a lark. Everything was forgotten, and we were like a pair of honeymoon lovers. Just as we were parting she said,

'There's a *fete* at Cordova; I shall go and see it, and then I shall know what people will be coming away with money, and I can warn you.'

"I let her go. When I was alone I thought about the *fete*, and about the change in Carmen's temper. 'She must have avenged herself already,' said I to myself, 'since she was the first to make our quarrel up.' A peasant told me there was to be bull-fighting at Cordova. Then my blood began to boil, and I went off like a madman straight to the bull-ring. I had Lucas pointed out to me, and on the bench, just beside the barrier, I recognised Carmen. One glance at her was enough to turn my suspicion into certainty. When the first bull appeared Lucas began, as I had expected to play the agreeable; he snatched the cockade off the bull and presented it to Carmen, who put it in her hair at once.[35]

"The bull avenged me. Lucas was knocked down, with his horse on his chest, and the bull on top of both of them. I looked for Carmen, she had disappeared from her place already. I couldn't get out of mine, and I was obliged to wait until the bull-fight was over. Then I went off to that house you already know, and waited there quietly all that evening and part of the night. Toward two o'clock in the morning Carmen

[35]La divisa. A knot of ribbon, the colour of which indicates the pasturage from which each bull comes. This knot of ribbon is fastened into the bull's hide with a sort of hook, and it is considered the very height of gallantry to snatch it off the living beast and present it to a woman.

came back, and was rather surprised to see me.

"'Come with me,' said I.

"'Very well,' said she, 'let's be off.'

"I went and got my horse, and took her up behind me, and we travelled all the rest of the night without saying a word to each other. When daylight came we stopped at a lonely inn, not far from a hermitage. There I said to Carmen:

"'Listen—I forget everything, I won't mention anything to you. But swear one thing to me—that you'll come with me to America, and live there quietly!'

"'No,' said she, in a sulky voice, 'I won't go to America—I am very well here.'

"'That's because you're near Lucas. But be very sure that even if he gets well now, he won't make old bones. And, indeed, why should I quarrel with him? I'm tired of killing all your lovers; I'll kill you this time.'

"She looked at me steadily with her wild eyes, and then she said:

"'I've always thought you would kill me. The very first time I saw you I had just met a priest at the door of my house. And to-night, as we were going out of Cordova, didn't you see anything? A hare ran across the road between your horse's feet. It is fate.'

"'Carmencita,' I asked, 'don't you love me any more?'

"She gave me no answer, she was sitting cross-legged on a mat, making marks on the ground with her finger.

"'Let us change our life, Carmen,' said I imploringly. 'Let us go away and live somewhere we shall never be parted. You know we have a hundred and twenty gold ounces buried under an oak not far from here, and then we have more money with Ben-Joseph the Jew.'

"She began to smile, and then she said, 'Me first, and then you. I know it will happen like that.'

"'Think about it,' said I. 'I've come to the end of my patience and my courage. Make up your mind—or else I must make up mine.'

"I left her alone and walked toward the hermitage. I found the hermit praying. I waited till his prayer was finished. I longed to pray myself, but I couldn't. When he rose up from his knees I went to him.

"'Father,' I said, 'will you pray for some one who is in great danger?'

"'I pray for every one who is afflicted,' he replied.

"'Can you say a mass for a soul which is perhaps about to go into the presence of its Maker?'

"'Yes,' he answered, looking hard at me.

"And as there was something strange about me, he tried to make me talk.

"'It seems to me that I have seen you somewhere,' said he.

"I laid a piastre on his bench.

"'When shall you say the mass?' said I.

"'In half an hour. The son of the innkeeper yonder is coming to serve it. Tell me, young man, haven't you something on your conscience that is tormenting you? Will you listen to a Christian's counsel?'

"I could hardly restrain my tears. I told him I would come back, and hurried away. I went and lay down on the grass until I heard the bell. Then I went back to the chapel, but I stayed outside it. When he had said the mass, I went back to the *venta*. I was hoping Carmen would have fled. She could have taken my horse and ridden away. But I found her there still. She did not choose that any one should say I had frightened her. While I had been away she had unfastened the hem of her gown and taken out the lead that weighted it; and now she was sitting before a table, looking into a bowl of water into which she had just thrown the lead she had melted. She was so busy with her spells that at first she didn't notice my return. Sometimes she would take out a bit of lead and turn it round every way with a melancholy look. Sometimes she would sing one of those magic songs, which invoke the help of Maria Padella, Don Pedro's mistress, who is said to have been the *Bari Crallisa*—the great gipsy queen.[36]

---

[36] Maria Padella was accused of having bewitched Don Pedro. According to one popular tradition she presented Queen Blanche of Bourbon with a golden girdle which, in the eyes of the bewitched king, took on the appearance of a living snake. Hence the repugnance he always showed toward the unhappy princess.

"'Carmen,' I said to her, 'will you come with me?'
She rose, threw away her wooden bowl, and put her
mantilla over her head ready to start. My horse was
led up, she mounted behind me, and we rode away.

"After we had gone a little distance I said to her,
'So, my Carmen, you are quite ready to follow me,
isn't that so?'

"She answered, 'Yes, I'll follow you, even to death—
but I won't live with you any more.'

"We had reached a lonely gorge. I stopped my
horse.

"'Is this the place?' she said.

"And with a spring she reached the ground. She
took off her mantilla and threw it at her feet, and
stood motionless, with one hand on her hip, looking
at me steadily.

"'You mean to kill me, I see that well,' said she. 'It
is fate. But you'll never make me give in.'

"I said to her: 'Be rational, I implore you; listen to
me. All the past is forgotten. Yet you know it is you
who have been my ruin—it is because of you that I
am a robber and a murderer. Carmen, my Carmen,
let me save you, and save myself with you.'

"'Jose,' she answered, 'what you ask is impossible.
I don't love you any more. You love me still, and that
is why you want to kill me. If I liked, I might tell you
some other lie, but I don't choose to give myself the
trouble. Everything is over between us two. You are

my *rom*, and you have the right to kill your *romi*, but Carmen will always be free. A *calli* she was born, and a *calli* she'll die.'

"'Then, you love Lucas?' I asked.

"'Yes, I have loved him—as I loved you—for an instant—less than I loved you, perhaps. But now I don't love anything, and I hate myself for ever having loved you.'

"I cast myself at her feet, I seized her hands, I watered them with my tears, I reminded her of all the happy moments we had spent together, I offered to continue my brigand's life, if that would please her. Everything, sir, everything—I offered her everything if she would only love me again.

"She said:

"'Love you again? That's not possible! Live with you? I will not do it!'

"I was wild with fury. I drew my knife, I would have had her look frightened, and sue for mercy— but that woman was a demon.

"I cried, 'For the last time I ask you. Will you stay with me?'

"'No! no! no!' she said, and she stamped her foot.

"Then she pulled a ring I had given her off her finger, and cast it into the brushwood.

"I struck her twice over—I had taken Garcia's knife, because I had broken my own. At the second thrust she fell without a sound. It seems to me that I can still see her great black eyes staring at me. Then they grew dim and the lids closed.

"For a good hour I lay there prostrate beside her corpse. Then I recollected that Carmen had often told me that she would like to lie buried in a wood. I dug a grave for her with my knife and laid her in it. I hunted about a long time for her ring, and I found it at last. I put it into the grave beside her, with a little cross—perhaps I did wrong. Then I got upon my horse, galloped to Cordova, and gave myself up at the nearest guard-room. I told them I had killed Carmen, but I would not tell them where her body was. That hermit was a holy man! He prayed for her—he said a mass for her soul. Poor child! It's the *calle* who are to blame for having brought her up as they did."

CHAPTER IV

Spain is one of the countries in which those nomads, scattered all over Europe, and known as Bohemians, Gitanas, Gipsies, Ziegeuner, and so forth, are now to be found in the greatest numbers. Most of these people live, or rather wander hither and thither, in the southern and eastern provinces of Spain, in Andalusia, and Estramadura, in the kingdom of Murcia. There are a great many of them in Catalonia. These last frequently cross over into France and are to be seen at all our southern fairs. The men generally call themselves grooms, horse doctors, mule-clippers; to these trades they add the mending of saucepans and brass utensils, not to mention smuggling and other illicit practices. The women tell fortunes, beg, and sell all sorts of drugs, some of which are innocent, while some are not. The physical characteristics of the gipsies are more easily distinguished then described, and when you have known one, you should be able to recognise a member of the race among a thousand other men. It is by their physiognomy and expression, especially, that they differ from the other inhabitants of the same country. Their complexion is exceedingly swarthy, always darker than that of the race among whom they live. Hence the name of *cale* (blacks) which they frequently apply to themselves.[1] Their eyes, set with a decided slant, are large, very black, and shaded by long and heavy lashes. Their glance can only be compared to that of a wild creature. It is full at once of boldness and shyness, and in this respect their eyes are a fair indication of their national character, which is cunning, bold, but with "the natural fear of blows," like Panurge. Most of the men are strapping fellows, slight and active. I don't think I ever saw a gipsy who had grown fat. In Germany the gipsy women are often very pretty; but beauty is very uncommon among the Spanish gitanas. When very young, they may pass as being attractive in their ugliness, but once they have reached motherhood, they become absolutely repulsive. The filthiness of both sexes is incredible, and no one who has not seen a gipsy matron's hair can form any conception of what it is, not even if he conjures up the roughest, the greasiest, and the dustiest heads imaginable. In some of the large Andalusian towns certain of the gipsy girls, somewhat better looking than their fellows, will take more care of their personal appearance. These go out and earn money by performing dances strongly resembling those forbidden at our public balls in carnival time. An English missionary,

---

[1]It has struck me that the German gipsies, though they thoroughly understand the word cale, do not care to be called by that name. Among themselves they always use the designation Romane tchave.

Mr. Borrow, the author of two very interesting works on the Spanish gipsies, whom he undertook to convert on behalf of the Bible Society, declares there is no instance of any gitana showing the smallest weakness for a man not belonging to her own race. The praise he bestows upon their chastity strikes me as being exceedingly exaggerated. In the first place, the great majority are in the position of the ugly woman described by Ovid, "*Casta quam nemo rogavit.*" As for the pretty ones, they are, like all Spanish women, very fastidious in choosing their lovers. Their fancy must be taken, and their favour must be earned. Mr. Borrow quotes, in proof of their virtue, one trait which does honour to his own, and especially to his simplicity: he declares that an immoral man of his acquaintance offered several gold ounces to a pretty gitana, and offered them in vain. An Andalusian, to whom I retailed this anecdote, asserted that the immoral man in question would have been far more successful if he had shown the girl two or three piastres, and that to offer gold ounces to a gipsy was as poor a method of persuasion as to promise a couple of millions to a tavern wench. However that may be, it is certain that the gitana shows the most extraordinary devotion to her husband. There is no danger and no suffering she will not brave, to help him in his need. One of the names which the gipsies apply to themselves, *Rome*, or "the married couple," seems to me a proof of their racial respect for the married state. Speaking generally, it may be asserted that their chief virtue is their patriotism—if we may thus describe the fidelity they observe in all their relations with persons of the same origin as their own, their readiness to help one another, and the inviolable secrecy which they keep for each other's benefit, in all compromising matters. And indeed something of the same sort may be noticed in all mysterious associations which are beyond the pale of the law.

Some months ago, I paid a visit to a gipsy tribe in the Vosges country. In the hut of an old woman, the oldest member of the tribe, I found a gipsy, in no way related to the family, who was sick of a mortal disease. The man had left a hospital, where he was well cared for, so that he might die among his own people. For thirteen weeks he had been lying in bed in their encampment, and receiving far better treatment than any of the sons and sons-in-law who shared his shelter. He had a good bed made of straw and moss, and sheets that were tolerably white, whereas all the rest of the family, which numbered eleven persons, slept on planks three feet long. So much for their hospitality. This very same woman, humane as was her treatment of her guest said to me constantly before the sick man: "*Singo, singo, homte hi mulo.*" "Soon, soon he must die!" After all, these people live such miserable lives, that a reference to the approach of death can have no terrors for them.

One remarkable feature in the gipsy character is their indifference about religion. Not that they are strong-minded or sceptical. They have never made any profession of atheism. Far from that, indeed, the religion of the country which they inhabit is always theirs; but they change their religion when they change the country of their residence. They are equally free from the superstitions which replace religious feeling in the minds of the vulgar. How, indeed, can superstition exist among a race which, as a rule, makes its livelihood out of the credulity of others? Nevertheless, I have remarked a particular horror of touching a corpse among the Spanish gipsies. Very few of these could be induced to carry a dead man to his grave, even if they were paid for it.

I have said that most gipsy women undertake to tell fortunes. They do this very successfully. But they find a much greater source of profit in the sale of charms and love-philters. Not only do they supply toads' claws to hold fickle hearts, and powdered loadstone to kindle love in cold ones, but if necessity arises, they can use mighty incantations, which force the devil to lend them his aid. Last year the following story was related to me by a Spanish lady. She was walking one day along the *Calle d'Alcala*, feeling very sad and anxious. A gipsy woman who was squatting on the pavement called out to her, "My pretty lady, your lover has played you false!" (It was quite true.) "Shall I get him back for you?" My readers will imagine with what joy the proposal was accepted, and how complete was the confidence inspired by a person who could thus guess the inmost secrets of the heart. As it would have been impossible to proceed to perform the operations of magic in the most crowded street in Madrid, a meeting was arranged for the next day. "Nothing will be easier than to bring back the faithless one to your feet!" said the gitana. "Do you happen to have a handkerchief, a scarf, or a mantilla, that he gave you?" A silken scarf was handed her. "Now sew a piastre into one corner of the scarf with crimson silk—sew half a piastre into another corner— sew a peseta here—and a two-real piece there; then, in the middle you must sew a gold coin—a doubloon would be best." The doubloon and all the other coins were duly sewn in. "Now give me the scarf, and I'll take it to the Campo Santo when midnight strikes. You come along with me, if you want to see a fine piece of witchcraft. I promise you shall see the man you love to-morrow!" The gipsy departed alone for the Campo Santo, since my Spanish friend was too much afraid of witchcraft to go there with her. I leave my readers to guess whether my poor forsaken lady ever saw her lover, or her scarf, again.

In spite of their poverty and the sort of aversion they inspire, the gipsies are treated with a certain amount of consideration by the more ignorant folk, and they are very proud of it. They feel themselves to be a superior race as regards intelligence, and they heartily despise the people whose hospitality they enjoy. "These Gentiles are so stupid," said one of the Vosges gipsies to me, "that there is no credit in taking them in. The other day a peasant woman called out to me in the street. I went into her house. Her stove smoked and she asked me to give her a charm to cure it. First of all I made her give me a good bit of bacon, and then I began to mumble a few words in *Romany*. 'You're a fool,' I said, 'you were born a fool, and you'll die a fool!' When I had got near the door I said to her, in good German, 'The most certain way of keeping your stove from smoking is not to light any fire in it!' and then I took to my heels."

The history of the gipsies is still a problem. We know, indeed, that their first bands, which were few and far between, appeared in Eastern Europe towards the beginning of the fifteenth century. But nobody can tell whence they started, or why they came to Europe, and, what is still more extraordinary, no one knows how they multiplied, within a short time, and in so prodigious a fashion, and in several countries, all very remote from each other. The gipsies themselves have preserved no tradition whatsoever as to their origin, and though most of them do speak of Egypt as their original fatherland, that is only because they have adopted a very ancient fable respecting their race.

Most of the Orientalists who have studied the gipsy language believe that the cradle of the race was in India. It appears, in fact, that many of the roots and grammatical forms of the *Romany* tongue are to be found in idioms derived from the Sanskrit. As may be imagined, the gipsies, during their long wanderings, have adopted many foreign words. In every *Romany* dialect a number of Greek words appear.

At the present day the gipsies have almost as many dialects as there are separate hordes of their race. Everywhere, they speak the language of the country they inhabit more easily than their own idiom, which they seldom use, except with the object of conversing freely before strangers. A comparison of the dialect of the German gipsies with that used by the Spanish gipsies, who have held no communication with each other for several centuries, reveals the existence of a great number of words common to both. But everywhere the original language is notably affected, though in different degrees, by its contact with the more cultivated languages into the use of which the nomads have been forced. German in one case and Spanish in the other have so modified the *Romany* groundwork that it would not be possible for a gipsy from the Black Forest to converse with one of his Andalusian brothers, although a few sentences on each side would suffice to convince them that each was speaking a dialect of the same language. Certain words in very frequent use are, I believe, common to every dialect. Thus, in every vocabulary which I have been able to consult, *pani* means water, *manro* means bread, *mas* stands for meat, and *lon* for salt.

The nouns of number are almost the same in every case. The German dialect seems to me much purer than the Spanish, for it has preserved numbers of the primitive grammatical forms, whereas the Gitanos have adopted those of the Castilian tongue. Nevertheless, some words are an exception, as though to prove that the language was originally common to all. The preterite of the German dialect is formed by adding *ium* to the imperative, which is always the root of the verb. In the Spanish *Romany* the verbs are all conjugated on the model of the first conjugation of the Castilian verbs. From *jamar*, the infinitive of "to eat," the regular conjugation should be *jame*, "I have eaten." From *lillar*, "to take," *lille*, "I have taken." Yet, some old gipsies say, as an exception, *jayon* and *lillon*. I am not acquainted with any other verbs which have preserved this ancient form.

While I am thus showing off my small acquaintance with the *Romany* language, I must notice a few words of French slang which our thieves have borrowed from the gipsies. From *Les Mysteres de*

Paris honest folk have learned that the word *chourin* means "a knife." This is pure *Romany*—*tchouri* is one of the words which is common to every dialect. Monsieur Vidocq calls a horse *gres*—this again is a gipsy word—*gras*, *gre*, *graste*, and *gris*. Add to this the word *romanichel*, by which the gipsies are described in Parisian slang. This is a corruption of *romane tchave*—"gipsy lads." But a piece of etymology of which I am really proud is that of the word *frimousse*, "face," "countenance"—a word which every schoolboy uses, or did use, in my time. Note, in the first place, the Oudin, in his curious dictionary, published in 1640, wrote the word *firlimouse*. Now in *Romany*, *firla*, or *fila*, stands for "face," and has the same meaning—it is exactly the *os* of the Latins. The combination of *firlamui* was instantly understood by a genuine gipsy, and I believe it to be true to the spirit of the gipsy language.

I have surely said enough to give the readers of Carmen a favourable idea of my *Romany* studies. I will conclude with the following proverb, which comes in very appropriately: *En retudi panda nasti abela macha.* "Between closed lips no fly can pass."

THE END

Made in the USA
Las Vegas, NV
06 January 2022

40619103R00059